THE KING OF COALMAN'S HILL

By Matt Shea

"The King of Coalman's Hill," by Matt Shea.
ISBN 978-1-62137-748-1 (Softcover); 978-1-62137-749-8 (eBook).

Published 2015 by Virtualbookworm.com Publishing Inc., P.O.
Box 9949, College Station, TX , 77842, US.

Dedication

JANENE MARIE ANKARBERG is by far one of the most special people I've ever met. In fact, we were even married at one time! We are all familiar with that 'good kid' who worked at the local convenient store in town. (*Her own* 7-eleven store!) The smiling face full of enthusiasm that everyone fell in love with.

With pride she greeted customers and made sure there was always enough fresh coffee for everyone. Jerry Lewis fundraisers, softball team sponsorships and car washes for good causes are just a few of the fun-filled events that were known to happen through her store. Always spirited, she would dress up like something out of a Boris Karloff movie on Halloween *while serving her loyal customers at the store!*

Her children, Laura and Jessie, could not have asked for a *better* mom. Janene's husband, Ron, along with her mother, Karen, and brother, Travis, all had a better life because of her.

All good things must come to an end.

Janene was advanced to Heaven on December 31, 2014, with her legacy continuing. Her memory has saturated all of us with a feeling that she is still very much in our lives — *just managing a bigger store.*

In honor of the many lives she touched and the happiness she brought, I hereby dedicate this book to:

Janene Marie Ankarberg

Janene and her world-class smile.

The song has ended, but the melody lingers on.

Irving Berlin

A Special Thanks To Our Friend, Ric!

I AM ONE OF MANY who have felt a personal bond with *This Week in America* host Ric Bratton throughout the years. For me, he filled the shoes vacated by Paul Harvey and Johnny Carson. The familiar jingle that plays while his big brother voice takes over the airwaves has always brought out the child in me.

Whether he's interviewing an icon in the entertainment industry or a fellow unknown starving artist who expresses himself through good will, it's all good. That's because *everyone* is special to Ric Bratton, regardless of fame.

Somewhere out there, someone contacted Ric and brought my writings to his attention. From there, he took the fight to us. On more than one occasion, 'our' Ric allowed my daughter, Laura, Ella Ray, Renée Klause and me to share center stage with him—a *gift* that allowed the whole world to hear our story.

The immortal Andy Warhol quote about being famous in America for fifteen minutes definitely applies when it comes to knowing Ric.

This is my eighth publication and the four of us will celebrate the new book followed by a toast to *This Week in America* and our friend, Ric Bratton.

Ric, you have put wind in our sails and have done something outstanding for which we will always feel indebted. When we listen to your program we get to say:

That's our friend, Ric!

Thanks for the boost you have given us and keep up the great broadcasting!

Your friends:

Laura, Renée, Ella and Matt

Table of Contents

Chapter 1

ON COALMAN'S HILL, a lone snowflake fluttered from the sky in silence.

The humble soul of Clayton Graves watched as he cast a wish. The paper-thin fragment continued to sway in a balanced rhythm as it fell to the Earth. Finally the ice crystal landed on a lone tree stump where he and his childhood friends once gathered. A few more flakes followed gracefully, and then a few more...

Soon the intensity of a heavenly pillow fight broke out. With gratitude, the sixty-two-year-old African American raised his arms toward the sky with praise. Slowly, he turned in circles with mouth wide open and tongue sticking out to catch snowflakes. The child in Clayton Graves was still alive!

A prayer had been answered—Christmas time was refusing to leave.

The winter wonderland was receiving yet another layer of precious snow, taking the valley further back through time. Slopes of polished ice continue to rule the land, and firewood remained the gold standard. Internal combustion engines were of no use as yesterday's sleighs were summoned to duty—a necessary means to haul hay, provisions, or transport family members to church.

Every child's dream, both young and old, had come true, with the most cherished gift being granted: no school.

Clayton Graves stood tall, dressed in his battle gear. A billowing red nylon ski jacket with a worn camouflage jumpsuit and army-issued snow boots adorned the retired soldier. Around his neck was a lengthy plaid neck scarf that personified the heroic fighter pilot who lived in every boy. A matching pair of gray woolen mittens and beanie provided additional warmth against the winter cold.

It was now time to face a challenge that dated back to his childhood. With stopwatch in hand, he looked down at the vintage Flexible Flyer sled that his grandfather had gotten for Christmas generations ago. Written across its deck in faded black paint was *The Graves Express*, a display that illustrated family pride.

The spirited old man puffed out his chest, and with good reason. He held bragging rights from a past accomplishment. Clayton was once *The King of Coalman's Hill*, a title that he'd vowed to regain. One that he lost to a childhood friend named Hoarse Parker many years ago.

Clayton picked up the rope that was tied to the steering arms and marched ahead, taking methodical steps. His heavy boots crunched in the fresh snow. He was approaching the starting line, where the best of the best were timed sledding down Coalman's Hill. The designated starting line was where the old stump protruded from the ground. This was the 'meeting place' whenever his friends needed to discuss something in private. It was also where champions were crowned.

The finish line was almost one hundred and fifty yards down the steep hill. It was an imaginary line where a rickety old wooden gate had stood open for over a hundred years. It served as the back entrance to the coal mine that once flourished here.

Mysteriously, there was a massive metal plate that was equal to the side of a house just before the gate's opening. Clayton and his friends had always wondered why it was there.

Was it protecting a secret entrance to something important?

Was it an entryway to the center of the Earth?

Were people buried there?

2

Once they tried to lift a corner of it to look and see, but found that it was impossible to budge.

The iron plate did serve a purpose, however. It froze during the winter, allowing ice to form on its surface. This was crucial to anyone who challenged the title. The ice immediately increased one's speed like a bolt of lightning. Often, if a rider wasn't in true form, they would turn sideways and roll in the snow over and over again.

The gladiator trudged through the snow, pulling his steed. Looking at the stump, he gave a slight nod. This was to acknowledge the wonderful childhood he had with his buddies. They were a close-knit group of guys who were always there for one another. Friends that had passed away years ago, and were forever embedded in Clayton's mind. Watching the snowflakes swirl around the old stump brought back fond memories...

There was Charles Franklin; a tall, lanky friend he'd met at a church function when he was seven. Charles always had a smile on his face and offered encouragement to everyone. They were teammates in basketball, with Clayton always leading in assists. Charles died one Easter morning of a heart attack.

Earl Black would be there. He was affectionately nicknamed "Blackie" despite being the only white playmate in his social group. Earl was small in stature, but with his wild blond hair and energetic play was always guaranteed fun! Earl died while trying to save a boy from drowning.

Rolland White, alias "Whitie," never missed an outing. He was the largest boy in the group, but would never hurt a fly. If there was ever a discrepancy with other boys, Rolland's warm diplomacy would always prevail. He went on to be a pastor and youth counselor. One day he was diagnosed with diabetes, and shortly after that, went to the Lord.

Ever-present would be Carlton Jennings, the class clown. Carlton's pranks never stopped, but were always harmless. It was just his way of saying, "hi!" Carlton was always the first

3

one to share whenever he had candy. He would go on to be the group's first casualty. Carlton enlisted in the Army after high school and was soon reported missing in action.

The brother team of Daryl and Melvin Cooke were inseparable, with little brother, Melvin always trying extra hard to gain Daryl's approval. This drove Melvin to great success, as he would go on to become the county's first African-American police chief. Tragically, the good man who never touched alcohol was killed by a drunk driver during the holidays. His brother Daryl lived until he was almost sixty.

Last would be Hoarse Parker; his best friend and worst competitor. Hoarse was the most athletic boy in school, and pushed Clayton to excel in sports and in life. In football he relied on Clayton for key blocks and scolded him profusely whenever he failed. Many times Clayton sacrificed his body allowing Hoarse to score. It was as if they were brothers.

The all-city running back currently held the quickest time down Coalman's Hill—an unbelievable 23 seconds!

Looking at the lonely stump was a grim reminder of the present reality. Still, the memories would always be ingrained in Clayton's soul. Often a peculiar quirk of nature would suggest that they were all present, cheering on their friend to achieve a record time. Sometimes a slight whisper of wind would dust a fine mist of snow on him. It was the tradition he and his friends held before a run; wishing the rider good luck with a shower of snow. A gentle breeze through barren trees would create this sprinkling without disturbing anything else...

There were times when he thought he'd misplaced his gloves, only to find them inside a hollowed-out knot on the side of the stump. At one time they hid messages there and covered them with leaves. Then there were the times when he simply felt their presence and just *had* to wave back.

At the official starting line, a motivated Clayton Graves let go of the rope. His adrenaline started to mount as his

4

breath pulsated with a fog-like vapor resembling a locomotive gaining speed. He stared down the field blanketed with fresh snow. The course was a switchback-type path with a few offsetting curves that scaled the back side of the old coal mine. The trail held a glossy shine along the packed snow and ice from the many who glided down and climbed back up the hill. In essence, it was a slalom that allowed their sleds to travel at dangerous speeds; for those who dared...

The warrior that lives in every competitor was alive and well inside Clayton Graves. His last attempt had fallen short of the record time by a mere six seconds! The long walk up the slope had him inspect every turn and bump that had cost him precious time. From there, he would plot out his next attempt to ensure a better run.

Once home; *The Graves Express* would go through a thorough inspection. The cherished heirloom handed down by his father would be meticulously dried off and closely viewed at all angles. Sometimes the frame was bent or a board had come lose. All would be repaired as good as new, with steel wool being used to smooth the metal surface it rode on. Lastly, the all-important wax was generously applied to the runners.

There was another aspect that was equally important: track conditions.

The early morning guaranteed a coating of ice over the glistening snow. This allowed some of the fastest times on Coalman's Hill to be recorded. The evening was also known to provide an even better condition, if the weather cooperated. A brief warming trend could partially melt the snow on the trail they raced sleds on, with cooler evening temperatures creating a polished ice finish. When such an occurrence took place, the slope was set for record runs.

It was early evening, and Clayton's sled was prepped and ready to go. Ideal conditions awaited in the newly formed ice that reflected the snowy sky.

Everything was ready.

It was now time to follow the protocol required to be crowned *The King Of Coalman's Hill*—a standard procedure where the participant lined up even with the stump at the crest of the hill.

They were to lay face down on their sled and remain motionless until given the signal. At that moment, they were allowed to push themselves once—a cue for the timer to be activated as they began their decent. Flurries of snow dust were thrown at the rider like rice at a wedding ceremony. Friends yelled encouragement and cheered their comrade on as he picked up speed approaching the first turn.

There was one last finishing touch needed to make a record run *official.*

The timepiece.

Clayton took off his right-hand glove and placed it in the pocket of his ski jacket. He then reached into his pant's pocket and felt a small metal disc with a fine chain fastened to it. He pulled it out to display a vintage stopwatch, and turned it around to view an inscription—one that always brought tears to the man's eyes. Tears that eventually turned into a smile beaming with pride and determination.

The letters etched on the back of the stopwatch read:

William Floyd Graves

It was his late uncle's watch from a war fought decades ago. Another priceless heirloom handed down from the Graves family line. This keepsake was honored by his friends and used exclusively to measure the time needed to be crowned *The King Of Coalman's Hill.*

The stage was set as Clayton positioned his sled at the edge of the hill. With stopwatch in hand, he lay down on the fastest sled from his grandfather's day and waited until he *sensed* he was authorized to go.

The moment of truth had come. With the snowfall mystically subsiding, Clayton knew that he was cleared to go.

In one motion, he extended both hands forward with the sacred stopwatch ever-so protected. Using his opened left hand and clenched fist, he clawed into the icy snow and activated the timer. The sled was launched utilizing a swimmer's stroke as Clayton embarked on his latest record attempt.

Carefully, the jockey positioned the wooden deck on rails for the first turn. With increasing speed he glided swiftly through the first obstacle, like an Olympian competing for the luge face-down. He entered the second turn immediately, dragging his left foot slightly to maintain stability. Again, he flew through the turn in expertise fashion. Straightening out the projectile, he dodged a few bumps of packed snow. Clayton took careful aim at the frozen plate that rapidly approached him. It had to be entered *just right,* or the ride would instantaneously get off-kilter, costing valuable seconds. He was now traveling down the fastest point of the course with everything on the line.

Gritting his teeth, he hung onto the steering arms. Clayton took a deep breath and froze in position, hoping to shoot over the solid ice and regain his title. The transition from riding on packed snow to pure ice proved to be too much on this attempt. The sudden lack of friction caused a surge of speed that telegraphed his approach was slightly off course.

As soon as the runners left the cushion of snow to ride on the hardness of winter ice, trouble began. Clayton began to veer left, causing him to instinctively drag the opposite foot and lean in the same direction—a desperate attempt to salvage the run. This technique allowed him to avert tragedy in exchange for costing precious seconds. The sled was reduced to a slower speed as it straightened out and coasted over the metal plate. At last, he crossed the finish line and stopped the watch.

The evening's setting sun was falling fast, with just enough light to see if our hero was victorious. He immediately steered into a snowbank to end the ride. With heart pumping and hopes alive, he got off the sled to see where the second hand had stopped. Breathing heavily, he anxiously held the timepiece close to his face and studied it.

His time: thirty-two seconds. Not quite as good as his best, and well off the current record-holder's mark of twenty-three seconds. He closed the protective shield over the glass face and held the watch with both hands.

"Darn!" he exclaimed, stomping his right foot on the ground and kicking up a mist of snow. He spun around in frustration. At that moment, a feeling of tranquility overcame him. He again reminded himself that he was the sole survivor of his childhood. Looking up to the heavens, he addressed those who cared. "Don't worry," he shouted, shaking the stopwatch at the clouds. "I'll get it next time!"

Clayton Graves put the antique watch back into his pant's pocket. Bending over, he picked up the rope tethered to his sled. The revitalized child began the arduous climb back home. Clayton would now survey the tracks left by the sled's runners. He methodically accessed every turn, every 'cut' he took to see where improvements could be made.

Eventually, he found himself on top of the hill. He stared at the old stump with a peculiar feeling that made him question whether his childhood friends were actually there. He shook his head toward them to convey his disappointment. Next, he displayed a facial expression followed by a jest that promised he'd do better on his next attempt.

Glancing to the far left, he saw what was once the home of the old coalmine's foreman. It was a two-story wooden structure adorned with a deck that stretched along the entire front. Its charm continued with a massive stone chimney to one side, and white lace curtains in every window.

The rustic structure was more than just a house, however. It was also an old bunkhouse where many could stay. Beds with partitions and additional portable beds filled the upstairs, where there was a lone bathroom and shower. Downstairs featured a dining room from the previous century. It was equipped with a long table and matching benches that resembled the Last Supper.

The entryway to this house hid its hotel aspect, appearing like a traditional American home. It boasted a kitchen, living room, dining room, three bedrooms and a bathroom. The integrity of the structure remained consistent, with matching polished wooden floors and walls. It was built as a permanent onsite residence for the coalmine's foreman, with the necessities for housing any worker in need.

This was where tired miners who sweated away long hours often stayed. Decades of working men, warm meals and stories in front of a roaring fire had filled this residence. When the coal plant went out of business, its legacy had continued. It had gone on to become home for a community-oriented family that also had an open-door policy. This household however, had added an extra touch. They held the distinction of being the first non-white citizens in the county.

They were known as the Graves family.

Chapter II

SPARKS FLEW UPWARD as Clayton placed another piece of dry alder in the fireplace. It snapped and popped as its earthy scent saturated the entire house. There were more inviting aromas coming from the kitchen. His renowned stew was on the back burner, with biscuits in the oven.

Carefully, he placed the protective screen in front of the fireplace and sat in his easy chair. Having already washed up and changed into dry clothing, the man of the house was comfortable.

Anticipation started to build as Clayton fidgeted. He loved company and knew that Stanley the horse would soon be there. Like Santa Claus delivering gifts, the tall, muscular black steed would arrive pulling the church's sleigh, piloted by none other than Pastor Moore himself. His precious cargo could range from just a few parishioners, to a whole wagon full.

Clayton was well-prepared, knowing that they would all spend the night. He'd carefully planned for the festivities by ensuring he would have enough food and clean bedding for everyone. Equally important, he'd prepared the stable for his horse, Cider, along with the visiting Stanley. Cider was built like Stanley, but with beautiful golden hair.

There would also be someone else who would make his happiness complete.

A special little someone was the most wonderful gift his life had ever received. That would be his seven-year-old granddaughter, Elizabeth—the grandchild he took custody of when his daughter, Angela, died giving birth. Elizabeth Marie Graves kept her grandfather young. In fact, she was being raised in the same house and played in the same fields as he did.

A framed picture taken of his wife and daughter rested on an end table near the fireplace. It was in the corner of the room and seemed to follow Clayton whenever he was present. They kept him company whenever he was alone. Every morning, he said "good morning" to his deceased wife and daughter. Whenever he was going through a trial, he would ask his wife, Grace for guidance.

"Well, I guess our Lord wanted you to keep your mother company," he would say to Angela while looking at their smiles. Grace died of breast cancer when their daughter was young. The constant memory of his wife and daughter was always close at hand.

Clayton stretched as he looked around the room at the many family portraits. On one wall was a picture of his early childhood. He'd just turned four when he posed with his proud parents. Even back then, his patented smile was always present.

One day the son addressed his mother with a complaint. He felt *cheated* being an only child, and asked, "How come I don't have any brothers and sisters?"

His mother had an immediate answer. Picking him up she asked, "Didn't God tell you? You were brought here to be everybody's big brother!" She then kissed her son on the cheek and hugged him. The wonderful news registered deep inside Clayton and made him feel good all over.

He would go on to live by those words. Clayton Charles Graves went on to join the Army. Private Graves immediately advanced in ranking and safely guided men to protect this country. He was always the first one in and the last one out—having never lost a soldier.

There was something more that he prayed for. It was to have the peace of mind of knowing that he and his men had never killed an enemy soldier. He just wanted to show *who* they were and *what* they were capable of doing. For Commander Graves, it was all meant to be a diplomatic exercise to illustrate what this country really stood for.

I just want everyone to make it home and improve this world, he would think to himself while in uniform.

His father, Charles Graves, added to his wife's comments. "Your life is like this house," he said. "This is God's house, and that's why your grandfather was able to buy it. Mr. Steele was his boss and practically gave it to him when the coal plant went out of business. That man was working for the Lord, because he knew that we would always accept anyone who needed a place to stay."

Clayton remembered that there were times when a family or a vagabond would stay with them for a while. *It really was God's house.*

Scanning the room, he saw pictures of grandparents, cousins, aunts and uncles. All of whom were gone. There was a festive touch throughout the living room, however: Elizabeth's artwork! Multicolored paintings, hand prints, and flowing ribbons with colored tissue decorated the entire house. Many times she couldn't wait to get home from school to give Papa' another special gift she made.

"Did you do this?" he would ask in his jolly voice. Elizabeth would smile ear-to-ear, nodding her head. "It's so beautiful!" he would add. Then he would hug her with his massive arms, saying, "I love you so much."

Finally, he looked straight ahead at the mantle above the fireplace. There, front and center, was the theme of the house. It was a picture of Clayton and Elizabeth, both smiling. The little girl laid claim to having the best man in the whole wide world as her papa! The love that existed between the two of them was immeasurable. It denied any pain from entering her life—like the pain that normally results from losing a mother, or not having a father accounted for...

Smiling at the picture, the guardian could only nod in approval. They were the last of the Graves family, but all was fine.

The tranquil moment was interrupted by the sound of joyous voices, accompanied by laughter. A whinny from an old plow horse followed, making Pastor Moore's arrival unmistakable. Clayton got up from his chair and looked out the window. To his delight, he saw the holy man helping Elizabeth out of the sleigh. The big man opened the front door as his granddaughter ran up to him with open arms.

"Papa! Papa!" exclaimed the child. "I missed you!"

"Well, I missed you too," he replied as he picked her up. She kissed him on the cheek as many called out his name.

"Good evening, Clayton."

"Hi, Clayton."

"Clayton, it's great to see you."

This pleased Clayton, because he wanted to be on a first-name basis with everybody—regardless of age. Looking at the small crowd of friends carrying overnight bags, he realized that every seat in the sleigh must have been taken. Nobody ever passed up an opportunity to stay the night at Clayton Graves' house! "I have dinner waiting for everyone," announced the gentle giant. "Please come inside and get yourselves warm. I'll put Stanley in the stable with Cider and join you in a few minutes."

Once inside, the guests took off their boots and placed them by the door, along with their luggage. After that, coats and other winter apparel were hung on a nearby coat rack, as chilled bodies hovered around the fireplace. Soon goose bumps disappeared and everyone found a seat.

Clayton returned from the stable, saying, "It looks like Cider and Stanley are having a slumber party, too!"

"Papa," called out Elizabeth.

"What is it, darling?" asked Clayton.

"My friends and I want to sled down the hill with you," she replied in an enthused voice. "Can we, Papa? Please, Papa, please?"

The granddaughter had a support group, with Johnny King, Sandra Hudson, Billy West and Gail Paradise stuffing the ballet box.

"Please, Clayton, please! Can we go?"

He looked at their parents and saw Cheshire grins giving nods of approval.

Clayton was a marked man, but he wouldn't have it any other way. If there was anyone who wanted a nighttime run down Coalman's Hill with friends, it was him.

"Let's get dressed for it, and we'll meet at the stump," said the sixty-two-year-old playmate.

"Yeah!" cheered the children as they bombarded the loving man with hugs.

Clayton turned to the parents and spoke. "Everyone knows their way around here," he said. "Dinner is on the stove, and the biscuits are in the oven. I also have plenty of milk and juice in the refrigerator. You all know where the plates, bowls, glasses and

13

silverware are," he instructed. "Don't be shy and make yourself at home. You might even want to eat in front of the fireplace and stay warm," suggested the accommodating host.

Before leaving, he reminded everyone about breakfast the following morning. "I'm making flapjacks from an old recipe my mother taught me," he said, rubbing his stomach.

It took no time at all for his friends to volunteer for kitchen duty. "I'll wash the dishes tonight," said Connie Hudson.

"...And I'll clean up after breakfast," vowed Lisa King.

Clayton gave a thumbs-up and left to get changed.

In no time at all, Elizabeth and her friends were bundled up and playing by the stump. Out of the darkness came a deep voice that made everyone turn. It was the masculine figure of Clayton Graves calling out, "Ho, ho, ho." He was pulling a toboggan that had *Property Of The Freeland Coalmine Company* stenciled on its deck. The children became ecstatic and screamed out with joy.

The big man arrived and positioned the snow bus at the edge of the slope. "Everyone assume your positions," ordered the former commander. This situation was nothing new for Elizabeth and her friends. They each had their assigned seating, with Clayton steering the ship. Elizabeth held the utmost important position. She would sit in the very front, where the wood curved inward like a candy cane. Her job was to serve as lookout. The seven-year-old loved playing this role. She knew that everyone's safety depended on her and, like her papa, would *never* let anyone down.

All knew what to do. Clayton climbed in after his granddaughter and inched closer to her. His chest was now supporting her back, with his strong legs straddling hers. He reached for the rope needed to steer the toboggan and waited for the others to board.

Next, Gail and Sandra got in and inched forward in the same fashion. Johnny and Billy would wait for Elizabeth's authorization before they pushed the toboggan.

Elizabeth peered over the wooden shield and surveyed the glistening path lit by the heavenly stars. The girl in a pink wool stocking cap carefully looked for any signs of danger. Turning her head from left to right and extending upward, she searched for anything that served as a red flag. Nothing, from a fallen branch to

14

a jackrabbit finding its way home, would be allowed to cause a mishap on her watch. She took the time to study her surroundings, just the way her papa taught her. She looked carefully as far as the night would allow. Once satisfied, she got comfortable and snuggled into her seat. With pink mittens firmly holding onto the bulkhead, she gave the order. "It's safe to go."

Gloved hands patted her shoulders as the boys pushed the jumbo sled. Immediately, Johnny jumped in, yelling, "I'm in!"

Last was Billy, giving a final shove as he climbed aboard. "I'm in!" he shouted.

The ride was secured and in motion.

"Wheeeee!" was the sound echoing through the night as the sextet entered the first turn. Clayton pulled hard to the left, and then hard to the right as bodies shifted with the ride.

With eyes wide open, he belted out a Tarzan-like call of the wild as he got ready for the next turn. He swayed the lengthy missile through the second turn with a cargo of screaming kids. Pulling tight on the reins, he straightened out the toboggan. They were now traveling at top speed as he swerved back and forth to avoid bumps.

The famous metal plate of ice was now in view and approaching fast. At once, the ride accelerated as if it had afterburners. After flying through the open gate, they found themselves on flat ground covered with fluffy snow that safely slowed them to a stop.

The nighttime ride had come to an end—but what a ride!

The crew got out and thanked Clayton over and over again, hugging their hero. Next, snow dust was thrown high into the air by everyone. This was a 'law' that Clayton had passed on Coalman's Hill. 'Snow dust' happened when a handful of snow was thrown into the air, and anyone willing got underneath it. Absolutely no one was ever allowed to throw a snowball at anyone. Clayton's rule.

Everyone celebrated the run by dancing under a harmless shower of snow dust.

Once the jubilation calmed down, they realized it was time to get back home. The procedure used was one of honor: girls were to ride in the toboggan, with the *men* pulling. Eagerly, Johnny and Billy helped Clayton pull as the girls got a second treat. The walk uphill was full of warm conversations, interesting questions, and stories that made everyone giggle.

Looking to the horizon, one could see a lone house lit up like a jack-o-lantern. Bright lights channeled through leaded glass windows, giving an amber hue. The warm colors were cast over snowy fields, serving as a beacon. This was what Clayton remembered as a child.

The pristine setting, with smoke billowing out of the chimney, possessed an aura of love. It generated a feeling that had gone unchanged for over one hundred years—a feeling that let everyone know that *all* were invited to enter and get warm by the fire. This was a special home that promised good friends, hearty food, and a cozy bed for the night.

For generations, many had found such comfort there. It was also undeniable that these very grounds held an inexplicable sensation of joy and brotherhood. It was as if those from past visits returned and never left...

Chapter III

ON THE FOLLOWING MORNING, five children fogged up a window that overlooked the valley. Their bedtime prayers seemed to be answered as gray clouds covered the sky, with more snow falling. Again the countryside was blanketed as far as the eye could see, without a footprint in sight. This guaranteed that school would be closed for at least a few more days.

Clayton had already been up for hours with a fire going and flapjacks on the griddle. The tantalizing aroma of fresh ground coffee and bacon peaked noses, beckoning everyone downstairs. The bunkhouse on Coalman's Hill was starting another day with little feet jumping up and down for joy.

Everyone ate breakfast at the medieval table in the old dining room. The feast was one of fellowship, spawning conversations that included everyone. Eventually, the day's itinerary was discussed. "My sleigh is full of dry wood and provisions I got from the PX," commented Clayton. "I also have extra blankets, coats, and tools needed to do any minor repair work," he added.

"That should be more than enough," replied Pastor Moore.

At least twice a week, Clayton visited the elderly who lived in the nearby hills. He always felt that it was his calling to be their neighbor and watch over them. He even got them to doctors' appointments and church services when deep snow had them hunkered down.

A battle plan was being formulated with the 'snow day' serving as a trump card. Addressing the children, Clayton suggested, "It would be great if you would join us."

All at once, ecstatic children raised their arms and yelled, "Yeah!"

Pastor Moore liked what he saw. The African American pastor of over twenty years nodded in approval. *I bet the Lord wanted them to miss school for this reason,* he thought to himself.

Clayton and the pastor were primed. The mission had received further grace. It would now come with most prized gift that seniors always cried for: The happiness of children coming to visit.

This would teach Elizabeth and her friends a very important lesson in life, a higher level of education that would surpass anything they could have learned in a classroom. They would discover that they could make a difference by spending time with those who were lonely. From there, they would get the shock of their lives, finding out that these very souls had so much to share.

The five children were briefed by Pastor Moore. "You'll never realize how happy you will make them," he said. "Your presence will be the most cherished gift they could possibly receive."

It was agreed that both Stanley and Cider would join forces. They would each partake in the crusade by hauling full sleighs. This day would serve as further testimony that prayers *do* get answered. In the highlands, the old and weary were not frightened. They knew that soon, Clayton Graves would be coming down their paths.

After breakfast, Pastor Moore and Clayton went to the stable to harness Cider and Stanley to the sleighs. Once they finished, the children were found dressed and ready to go. The procession was led by Clayton, wearing a ceremonial stovepipe hat like Abe Lincoln with red earmuffs. Together he and Elizabeth sat tall on the buckboard with runners as Pastor Moore's crew followed behind. With hot cider in a thermos and full paper cups, they left for the nearest household.

The caravan glided through the powdered snow. Occasionally they spotted a clearing with hungry sparrows searching for food. The members of the Freeland Community Church were well-prepared and had brought birdseed to spread their goodwill. Fistfuls were thrown, as chirping sounds acknowledged the handout.

Around the corner nestled a tiny cottage with smoke rising from the chimney. Peering out its view window was a silver-haired couple wearing matching red flannel shirts. Together they stood watch, looking at the sea of frozen crystal that separated them from the outside world. This was the home of Walter and Clara Rodman, a high school couple from the 1950s. They were marooned, with snowdrifts surrounding all sides. Despite being held captive by Jack Frost, they were warm and feared not. They had faith, knowing that the 'caretaker of the foothills' would not forget them.

The tranquil moment abruptly became one of celebration as the black knight in shining armor turned into their garage-way. Sitting tall was the all-loving smile of Clayton Graves, with a bundled-up Elizabeth riding shotgun. The cavalry arrived with provisions and something extra special.

They brought the makings of a family for the couple who never had children.

Clayton was always two steps ahead of the game and grabbed a snow shovel he kept under the bench seat. "Wait here until I clear the walkway," he said to his granddaughter. Pastor Moore was already parked behind Clayton's sleigh. He and the others remained seated and watched the mountain man clear a safe path.

Massive gloved hands gripped the shovel's handle as scoops of snow flew from side to side. Inside, the prom queen and her king watch their hero chucking snow as he slowly advanced toward their front door. Once finished, he politely tapped on the door. Walter and Clara opened it. The spirited man bowed as he removed his hat, saying, "Clayton Graves at your service."

The Rodmans were taken by his chivalry and were at a loss for words. Finally, Walter spoke. "Well, let's get everyone in here!"

Clara followed suit. "I'll make some coffee and hot chocolate."

Putting his hat back on, the big man smiled and said, "We'd love that!"

Clayton walked back to his sleigh and put the shovel underneath the seat. With one mighty swoop, he picked up Elizabeth and gently placed her on the ground. "You are going to make some old folks very happy today," he said in a cheerful tone. Next, he motioned with his right arm, signaling the others to join them.

Soon the living room was full, with no introductions needed. Everyone was already well-acquainted from church. There was something different this time, however. This was a special visit that stemmed from love and goodwill. It was a pilgrimage that led to their very own home, and they loved it! The household that never knew children had plenty that day.

"We're so happy to see you!" exclaimed the couple on social security.

Within minutes, Clayton and Pastor Moore excused themselves. They had food to bring in and firewood to stack. From there, they would quietly assess whether any minor repair work was needed and make doubly sure there were enough blankets and winter clothing. Last, Clayton would shovel a path around the one-bedroom house, preventing snow from covering the windows.

All of this took place while the boys were gathered around Walter, and the girls were in the kitchen with Clara.

Clayton and Pastor Moore verified that all was secured. They eventually found themselves warming up in the living room with a hot cup of coffee and great company.

The visit was winding down, as there were three other households to check up on. "You are welcome to stay longer," offered Clara Rodman in an emotional tone that almost pleaded.

"It's bad enough that we can't attend the weekly nighttime gatherings that normally happen at church," said Walter.

"They had to be canceled because of the snow," said Pastor Moore.

Clayton asked the pastor a question. "What if there was a way to get people there?" he asked.

Looking directly at Clayton, Pastor Moore gave his answer. "I'd gladly provide services, even if it was just for a few. They would also be more than welcome to stay the night."

Clara held Walter's hand in the hope that such an event would happen. Clayton looked at the couple and saw the youth inside them glowing.

Looking at the pastor, he asked, "How soon would you be willing to have an all-night sleepover at church?"

It took no time for the holy man to respond. "Right now!" he said, pounding his fist on a table.

The child inside Clayton took control. He was excited over the thought of having another sleepover with friends—a sleepover on a grander scale that would include the Rodmans and other stranded families. Standing up, he looked at the others and said, "Raise your hand if you want to have a stay-over at church tonight."

It was unanimous. All at once, everyone stood on their tiptoes and raised a waving hand, including Clayton. Plans were made, with the understanding that Clayton would be back before sunset.

Oh what fun they'll have on a one-horse open sleigh!

Stanley and Cider continued their trek, reaching the Lunds and Gilmores. Snow was shoveled; dry wood, blankets and food provided. An enchanted visit took place in both dwellings, with everyone wanting to go to the all-night spiritual party.

"We'll pick you up before sunset," Clayton promised each household.

There was one family left to drop in on: the Patterson's.

This visit always proved to be a little uncomfortable for the family of three. They were perched the furthest away and had learned one day that there was a family of color around.

Years ago, Clayton heard a noise late at night. It was coming from the side of his house and prompted him to investigate. What he saw was the father-and-son team of Wendell and Wendell Jr. with paint brushes in hand. Next to them was an open can of white paint. They were caught before any damage was done. A few words of hospitality and wisdom were conveyed by Clayton, and the intruders' tails went between their legs.

An understanding was made that evening, and handshakes were exchanged. Clayton went back to bed with nothing more ever being said about it. The Patterson's were on Clayton's good list, just like everyone else. Again, provisions were delivered with a friendly visit that included an offer to stay all night at the church.

They were touched by the offer and thought of the friends that would be there. Equally important, it would mean more time with Clayton and his granddaughter. They accepted with eagerness.

21

Wendell, along with his wife and son, formed a tight circle, hugging the big man. They thanked him for his big heart, saying, "We love you."

Clayton responded with sincere words.

"I love you, too."

He then stood at attention. Pointing his military index finger at the trio, he gave a command. "Be ready by sunset."

The Patterson's loved his determination. They stood at attention and saluted back.

The sleighs were now much lighter as they traveled back to the Graves' bunkhouse. By sunset they would be full again—with happy travelers, hot cider, and baked goodies, heading toward a spiritual evening.

Chapter IV

IT WAS NIGHTFALL in Freeman Valley.

Somewhere amongst the snow-covered evergreens was a matching roof with icicles. As one got closer, a steeple with lit stained glass windows could be seen. At once the joyous sounds of a choir erupted, spreading its glory throughout the wilderness. This was the Freeman Community Church, and there was life inside!

A last-minute effort created this moment—a labor of love brought forth by two God-fearing men. It was Clayton Graves chauffeuring a sleigh full of parishioners, while Pastor Moore prepared the church and making phone calls. These efforts paid off with huge dividends, allowing a substantial congregation to be assembled.

Most important, those considered out of reach were personally brought there.

The evening was a family event from the get-go. Pastor Moore initiated the services with a warm sermon, stressing how our Creator takes care of us despite any circumstances. Everyone nodded along, relating to his inspiring words. Afterward it became a social event in the church's rectory, with juice and warm finger food for all. The evening progressed with hot cider and a bonfire outside. Soon, all held hands and sang hymns around a massive Christmas tree that was still decorated with multicolored lights.

As promised, plenty of cots were available, along with heavy quilts and pillows. Breakfast would greet everyone the next morning, with a service to follow.

The next day saw the group that traveled with Pastor Moore return to their homes. Before leaving, they thanked Clayton and

Elizabeth for their hospitality, as many hugs and handshakes were exchanged.

"That house is always open to everyone," said Clayton. "Always feel free to stay with us."

Clayton and Elizabeth would now backtrack with their neighbors and return everyone to their prospective households. "I'll be by in a day or two to see how you're doing," he would say after each family was safely dropped off.

When they arrived at the last stop, there was something terribly wrong. A tree had fallen over, taking out the power lines to Walter and Clara's house.

True, Clayton had just loaded them up with dry wood—but that wouldn't be enough for the aging couple to survive. "Looks like you'll be staying with us for a while," he commented.

The Rodman's were overwhelmed by Clayton's compassion. They had survived winters because of him and always cherished his company. The last thing they wanted to be guilty of was imposing.

"We don't want to put you out in any way, Clayton," said Walter. "You have done so much for us already."

The big man had a firm answer. "Put me out?" he questioned in a high-pitched voice. "I would never be happy here if it wasn't for friends like you," he said. "Besides, that's not our house we're living in."

The couple gave Clayton a confused look as they tried to understand.

"It's God's house," he explained. "That place has always been meant for everybody. Elizabeth and I are just fortunate that it was there for us."

The elders digested what Clayton had said. They were all too familiar with the bunkhouse on Coalman's Hill. In fact, Walter had once worked there along with his father and grandfather. As he recalled, they had freezing nights where the house on Coalman's Hill took them in. Those were stays that included a warm meal with friends in front of the fireplace.

Suddenly it dawned on the old man that Clayton was right. That place on the hill *is* God's house, and he and his wife were always welcome there.

With conviction, Clayton Graves spoke. "The Lord has given me the honor of leading men into battle without ever losing a soldier." Taking a deep breath, he looked straight ahead and continued. "Well, this is another battle, and I'm not going to lose you either."

Elizabeth looked at her grandfather with pride. She remembered the many times he'd held her tight, promising that he'd always be there for her.

Excitement grew for the married couple. "We'll get packed and be here within ten minutes!" said Walter.

They were home half an hour later. Cider was taken to his stable, and the old plow horse began eating a well-deserved meal as Clayton patted him on the back, saying, "You took care of us again."

Once inside, it became obvious that Walter and Clara would have the entire upstairs to themselves. "This will work out just fine," said Clayton. "Elizabeth and I love having friends living here with us..."

It was natural for Clara to be drawn to Elizabeth. Throughout her entire life, she'd imagined how wonderful it would have been to have a daughter and share life together. On Coalman's Hill, her dream would come true for an indefinite amount of time.

The woman of the house gave Clara a personal grand tour that finished in the kitchen.

Appetites were building as an age-old dream crossed the old woman's mind. Looking down at the child, Clara placed her hands on her hips and acted like the mother she always wanted to be. Tapping her right foot on the floor, she addressed her 'daughter.'

"Ya know what sounds good?" she asked.

Elizabeth loved the moment. She was with a 'mommy' now and sensed that they were about to do something very special. With excitement, she asked, "What?"

"We have two hungry men that just put in a hard day," Clara pointed out. "Maybe you and I could cook them a dinner that they'll always remember," she suggested.

Elizabeth was thrilled at the thought of doing grownup stuff. All she could do was hug the mother figure and nod her head over and over again. Clara put her arms around her and held on.

Finally, she extended her arms while holding onto the child. Clara looked at Elizabeth with her loving face changing expressions. "Hey, we've got hungry men out there," she said. "We need to get started!"

"Can I tell them what we're going to do?" asked the seven-year-old.

"They would love that!" replied Clara.

The girls marched into the living room to find a usual male setting. With coffee cups in hand, the men enjoyed the warmth of a fire while fishing trophies increased in size through conversation. Elizabeth ended the competition by running up to her papa and standing in formation. Her loving brown eyes and involuntary smirk prepared Clayton for good news.

"What is it, darling?" he asked.

"Clara and I are going to make dinner for everyone!" she announced.

"Well, that's just wonderful," he replied.

Walter joined in. "How about letting an old Army cook bake some buns?"

"Oh," said his wife. "Your famous buns are to die for!"

Walter turned to Clayton and said, "Why don't you take a long-deserved rest while we *girls* work in the kitchen?"

Clayton was all smiles. "There's plenty in the refrigerator," he said. "Just help yourself."

Clayton walked into the kitchen as the others followed. He placed his coffee cup in the sink and said, "I'll find something to do."

"Take your time," said Clara. "We'll come up with something—just give us an hour and a half."

At that moment, a thought entered her mind.

In Clara's world, there was only one way to prepare chicken and dumplings, and this would be the perfect night for it. She quietly said a little prayer and searched the kitchen with hopes of finding the proper ingredients to resurrect this age-old family recipe. To her amazement, all was there, as if it were set aside just for this special evening: the fowl, vegetables, seasoning—everything.

This discovery would allow another dream to come true late in life. The sixty-six-year-old woman now had someone to pass this part of her heritage down to.

Soon Elizabeth was wearing oversized padded gloves as Clara mentored her. The newly formed 'mother-and-daughter' team was preparing chicken and dumplings for dinner!

The man of the house decided to go upstairs and see how his guests were situated for their stay. When he got there, he used two beds and a rolling partition, along with a dresser, lamp and nightstand, to create a cozy bedroom. Everything was already cleaned up and put away from the guests who'd stayed the night before. This consideration put a smile on his face as he walked toward a window to look out.

The sun was beginning to set, with more snow clouds moving in from the horizon. He looked at the old stump which was the focal point of his childhood and thought about his friends that always gathered there. Looking just beyond, he saw the winding trail that skyrocketed sleds to record speeds.

Winter winds had just transformed the icy course into a polished shine.

A *feeling* had come over him.

He was certain that his friends had made arrangements for him to see the updated conditions. It was obvious that they were *all* there, beckoning him to attempt another challenge.

Clayton was once again seeing a page out of his childhood. For whatever reason, those in the house would be preoccupied, allowing him to attend unfinished business with his old buddies.

Like a child sneaking around on Christmas Eve, he quietly entered his room, changed into his snow outfit and left the house undetected. Once outside, he went to his workshop out back and entered.

There before him was a workbench that held The Graves Express, with the precious stopwatch lying next to it. Clayton picked up the engraved watch and cautiously twisted its winding mechanism back and forth three times. Next he opened the tarnished covering that exposed its face and activated the timer. The second hand moved one increment at a time, stopping abruptly with each tick. All was in working order. He stopped the watch and reset it. With loving care, he closed the timepiece and placed it into his pocket.

He was now studying the former record holder. The Flexible Flyer from last century was true and balanced, having already been serviced. Waxed and ready to go he picked it up, tucked it under one arm and proceeded to the arena that awaited.

Clayton was positioned on his sled, waiting to be cleared for takeoff. He'd already greeted the 'guys' and was now poised to record the quickest run of his life. Or so he thought...

A slight gust of wind carried particles of snow like desert sand from the nearby trees. A fine mist formed, sprinkling the general area. It was time for Clayton to begin. He gave himself one push while activating the timer.

The ground was noticeably firm from the packed ice, allowing a good start. He flew through the first turn with ease and positioned himself for the second.

Clayton remembered that fateful day when Hoarse Parker shattered the old record. He did it by not dragging his right foot while speeding through the second turn—a tactic that only worked on one occasion. It's a gutsy move that practically guarantees disaster.

Clayton Graves knew that he was on record pace and decided to go for broke. The speed demon inside him elected to gamble with Hoarse's risky maneuver. Flying into the turn, he did nothing to slow down. His velocity caused him to leave the preferable lower track and elevated him to a wall of spongy snow. This poor miscalculation caused him to slow down drastically as he reached an angle that almost flipped him upside-down.

In sheer panic he dragged both feet, aimed the sled almost sideways and traveled to ground level. He successfully connected with the path of choice, but the attempted was already ruined. Clayton regained his composure and coasted straight ahead, dodging a few bumps and finally gliding over the metal plate. Once passing through the open gates, he stopped the timer and turned the sled into a fluffy mound. He got up, taking deep breaths. In frustration he looked at his time:

An embarrassing forty-one seconds.

He closed the stopwatch in shame and placed it back into his pocket. Looking up the hill, he yelled, "That was my fault, but I won't make that mistake again!"

Clayton was now more determined than ever. Shaking his fist toward the stump, he vowed, "I'll get it next time!" He began the climb back home, murmuring to himself. *If only I dragged my foot a little bit, I'd have the record now...*

Looking up, he saw the old bunkhouse with its lights shining like the Northern Star. A warm feeling generated inside Clayton. He was like many who had traveled up Coalman's Hill through the years. He knew that soon he would be inside with loved ones. From there an evening would take place consisting of a warm meal, the serenity of a fire, laughter, and some prayer.

Chapter V

THE GRAVES EXPRESS WAS NOW resting quietly in the workshop, to be attended to later.

The warrior had since re-entered the bunkhouse, taken a shower and changed. Suddenly, his body became more weary than usual. His recent escapade seemed to have taken an extra toll, telling him that he needed to lie down. In fact, the man had lost a bit of weight recently. Fully clothed, Clayton lay on top of his bed and closed his eyes.

At that moment a familiar tapping came from the door. "Papa," a soft voice called out.

Clayton was almost asleep when he heard his granddaughter. Immediately, he got out of bed and opened the door.

There before him stood his proud princess, wearing a kitchen apron. Her body language telegraphed that she was anxious to tell him something. At that instant, a hearty aroma tickled his nose, causing his stomach to growl.

The cat was out of the bag.

He remembered that she was helping Clara cook dinner. He also detected her feeling of accomplishment and didn't want to ruin the moment. Clayton pretended not to notice anything, allowing Elizabeth the honor of telling him the news.

"What is it, darling?" he gently replied.

The woman of the house began to quiver with excitement. Her bright eyes lit up as she said, "Clara and I made chicken and dumplings for dinner, and it's real good!"

Clayton tilted his head up and started to sniff. He illustrated that something wonderful had just tickled his nose, causing a major distraction—one that took control of his entire body. Closing his eyes, it appeared that the enticing scent placed him in a trance as he listed slightly back and forth under its spell.

Elizabeth loved it!

Finally, he snapped out of it, giving direct attention to his granddaughter. "Is that the dinner you and Clara made for us?" he questioned in astonishment.

The novice chef nodded repetitiously with her beautiful smile showing pride.

Later that evening, the dining room and kitchen were cleaned with everything put away. "I have never enjoyed such a great dinner in all my years!" exclaimed Clayton as he patted his full stomach.

"Well, good," replied Clara. "There are plenty of leftovers in the refrigerator, too."

"And Papa," added Elizabeth. "Clara taught me how to make chicken and dumplings the way her mother used to. Now I can make it for dinner whenever we want it!"

"Oh, that sounds good!" replied Clayton.

The evening was starting to slow down. The fresh wood placed in the fireplace cracked and popped, enriching the living room with its alder fragrance. Elizabeth was in her pajamas, when Clara began to ask questions about her life. "What do you and your papa do at nighttime?" she asked.

"I always do my homework first when I come home from school, and Papa checks it," she said. "Then we have dinner and share it with our friends who come by to visit," she added. "They know that they are also welcome to stay the night—and a lot of times, they do. It's always fun whenever anyone stays the night with us!" she exclaimed.

Clara smiled at the child, knowing that her comment was directed toward her and her husband. The elder hugged the child with both hands, realizing that they *were* friends.

Clara held on and marveled at how rich the little girl's life was. She was grateful to become a part of it. Letting go, she leaned back and asked, "What do your papa and you do when you're by yourselves ?"

"Papa and I have a lot of fun when we're by ourselves," she said, sticking her chest out. The second-grader began to elaborate:

"We talk, make each other laugh, watch TV, play checkers, and every night Papa reads me bedtime stories before we say our goodnight prayers."

What Elizabeth described was all Clara had ever wanted. The senior's heart was touched again as she hugged the precious child a second time. "Checkers," commented the denied mother. "I love playing checkers!"

"Let's play in the dining room!" exclaimed Elizabeth. "I'll get my checker set and meet you there."

The child came out in Clara. With enthusiasm she placed her hands on Elizabeth's shoulders and said, "Okay!"

The girls went on to play checkers and laugh from story to story until bedtime arrived.

In the meantime, Clayton and Walter watched from a distance and remained quiet. They were in awe witnessing a natural pairing between two souls; a bond between a mother and daughter that life had finally granted. This was clearly a spiritual act as a prayer from many years ago began to take form. Each man knew that this was God's hand in motion and understood not to interfere.

It was beautiful.

The evening was capped off with an extra push. It happened when Clayton noticed that it was getting late and entered the dining room. Looking at Clara, he made a suggestion. "Why don't you read Elizabeth some bedtime stories tonight? When you two are done, we can all say our goodnight prayers together."

That was music to Clara's ears! Her face lit up as she turned to Elizabeth. "Read as many as you'd like," Clayton added.

Elizabeth loved the idea and reciprocated by hugging Clara with all her might. The child who never knew her mother only wanted to get closer.

Chapter VI

CLAYTON GRAVES WAS AN EARLY bird who always woke up before sunrise, bright-eyed and bushy-tailed. This morning would prove to be different. He awoke with a nauseous feeling that included dizziness. It was a flu-like symptom that was somehow a little different. This was awkward for the man who normally carried the strength of two.

Me, sick? he thought to himself. *It couldn't have been what we ate last night. That meal was delicious; besides, everyone was fine after dinner...*

He sat up in bed and felt pain in his joints. Eventually his body perked up, allowing him to start his day. *Must be a bug going around,* he concluded. *I hope nobody else gets it...*

Downstairs was a different story. Clara woke up early and ever so slightly tapped on Elizabeth's door.

The child answered. "Yes...?"

Clara opened the door and saw Elizabeth sitting up in bed. She was warm and snuggled under a homemade quilt, with only her pretty face showing. Like herself, the child went to sleep knowing that someone very special had just entered her life. A special someone who addressed areas beyond what her papa could provide. It was the *woman* in her that was now being cultivated. She woke up early with the hunger to strengthen the bond that had been started.

"Good morning, Elizabeth," whispered Clara.

"Good morning, Clara," Elizabeth whispered back.

The child with rich Afro hair and a gorgeous smile wanted to be hugged. Extending her arms, she leaned toward Clara. The old woman took no time to respond. She woke up *needing* a hug as well. A hug that couldn't come from just anybody, though—she needed one from the daughter she never had.

The big girl took long strides to the open arms and hugged *her child* immensely. "I love you, Elizabeth," she said with all her heart.

"I love you too," answered the little girl. "Are we going to do anything today?" she asked.

Clara had her gun loaded. Leaning back, she locked eyes with Elizabeth's and whispered loudly, "Do you want to help me make breakfast this morning?" The girls were like-minded, and Elizabeth nodded her head with enthusiasm. Their eye contact held, with each knowing that they were in it together.

Clayton and Walter would eventually hear the sound of bacon and eggs frying, and smell fresh coffee in the air. "Men need a hearty breakfast," commented Clara to her protégé.

How right she was. Throughout breakfast, the men savored the meal while giving a non-stop barrage of compliments to the chefs. The setting was one of tranquility, with the foursome nestled in the warm dining room. Clayton looked out the window and noticed that another snow storm had started. "Looks like school will be delayed a bit longer," he said.

Elizabeth left the table and ran to the window. Looking up to the snowy sky, she raised both hands in victory.

"This would be a good day to crochet an afghan," said Clara.

Elizabeth quickly turned around. "Will you teach me how to crochet, Clara?"

"I'd love to," came the response. "In fact, I brought some yarn and hooks with me."

"Yeah!" screamed Elizabeth as she ran to Clara, hugging her. Clayton and Walter looked at each other. Without anything being said, they picked up their coffee mugs and gave a 'cheers'.

"I was going to load up my sleigh with firewood and canned food to check up on our neighbors today," said Clayton.

"That's a good idea," said Walter. "I'll help you."

"Don't worry about us," said Clara. "Elizabeth and I will clean the kitchen, and then we'll start crocheting."

"Well, it sounds like you two are going to have a good day together," said Clayton.

Breakfast came to an end, and the men got cleaned up. It was agreed that they would change into their snow outfits and meet in the stable. Once there, the first priority would be to feed Cider. Clayton filled his trough with a mixture of hay, apples, carrots and oats. Patting the draft horse on the side, he said, "We'll be needing you today, Cider."

Walter looked around and saw many shelves full of canned food. Next to them was an abundance of dry wood stacked neatly against a wall, with the sleigh alongside. "That's what keeps me in shape," commented Clayton.

"I'll start loading the sleigh," said Walter.

"Why don't you get inside the sleigh, and I'll hand the wood to you?" suggested Clayton. Walter gave a thumbs-up and assumed his position. The human assembly line got underway as pieces of split alder exchanged hands.

A rhythm was established, as the sleigh got steadily filled. Several minutes into the chore, Clayton became lightheaded and started to lose his balance. He abruptly stopped and placed a hand against the wood pile for stability. The man was beginning to feel weak, and perspired more than usual. Walter saw Clayton and became alarmed. "Are you all right?" he asked.

Clayton started to recover and said, "I seem to have caught a bug. Don't worry about me," he added, "I'm sure it's nothing that a good sweat couldn't cure."

The big man caught his breath and continued to shuffle wood—at a much slower rate.

Three households later, Clayton and Walter were gliding over the snow on a return trip. The scene would have made the perfect Christmas card.

There were two men on a sleigh pulled by a horse, with snow falling everywhere. Clayton's stovepipe hat, along with two neck scarves fluttering in the gentle breeze, took one back through time.

"I think everyone has enough firewood for a while," said Walter laughingly.

"And food," added Clayton. The empty sleigh put a thought in his mind. "Let's check up on your place," he suggested. "Maybe you would like to get a few more things to bring back."

"That's a good idea," said Walter.

They rode a little further and turned into the driveway of the old cottage. What they saw made time stand still. The windows were now sheets of ice, and the chimney was encased in snow. It appeared as if no one had ever lived there. *Thank God they're with us,* thought Clayton.

Walter gazed at his home, realizing that he and his wife had been saved. Taking a deep breath, he said, "Wait here, I'll only be getting a few things." He entered his house as Clayton looked skyward.

Soft flakes continued to fall, casting serenity far and wide. It encompassed everything and brought with it a feeling of knowing that everyone was safe and secure in God's hands.

Clayton felt compelled to speak out as the heavenly flakes touched his face. "Gracie, Angie; I bet you two are behind all of this..."

Walter returned with a cardboard box full of miscellaneous items, ranging from toothpaste to an extra set of matching pajamas. Their brisk ride through the gentle snowfall continued as they made their way to Coalman's Hill.

The men arrived back home and promptly put Cider into its stable. The steed was rewarded for its service by being fed apples and brushed. Inside, another treat awaited. Clara had taught Elizabeth how to make homemade vegetable beef soup and baked bread. This was *their* reward for taking care of others. "Your papa is such a good man," said Clara. "I don't think that we would have survived this winter without him."

How right she was...

The men entered the house and placed their hats, scarves and coats on the coat rack. Next they took off their boots and set them by the door. Before they had a chance to think, the hearty smell of another warm meal overwhelmed them. Clayton was raised with such tantalizing aromas making their way through the kitchen. These scents of select spices and seasoning always promised to make friends and visitors alike feel welcome.

This time, things were a little different. The kitchen had a new tag team at work—and their creations were out of this world! The newly formed mother-and-daughter combo was utilizing Clara's secret family cookbook, adding a touch of their own. The girls were doing their part to keep up the tradition of Coalman's Hill by cooking in bulk, in the event that anyone came to their door cold and hungry.

It was the Graves' family signature.

Clara's voice could be heard from the kitchen. "Lunch will be served in five minutes."

It didn't take long for two hungry men to get washed up and seated at the kitchen table. To their surprise, a subtle presentation would also be included.

Elizabeth was wearing a new hairstyle with a pretty blue ribbon placed 'just right' off to one side. Her new look, ever-present smile and breathtaking eyes belonged on a magazine cover.

"My, oh my," exclaimed her papa. "Every boy in the valley will be here wanting to court you."

Lunch was served with a touch of class. Elizabeth's beauty set the tempo, with the stew served in a shiny brass tureen. "Where did you find that?" asked her grandfather. "My mama use to serve her homemade cranberry sauce in it during the holidays."

"It was wrapped in paper and buried in the far corner, where the pots and pans are kept," said Clara.

"Mercy!" exclaimed Clayton. "This place keeps getting more life!"

Another meal was shared at the Graves' home with repetitive compliments to the chefs. Throughout the meal, Elizabeth's loving eyes continuously stared at the man she loved. The hearty stew with biscuits and her updated beauty didn't require any words. Clara eventually asked questions about the men's recent visits.

"They're all just fine and send their regards to you and Elizabeth," said Walter.

"Did you stop by our house?" she asked.

That question made her husband wince. Sitting back in his chair, he looked up with his eyes rolling around. It was obvious that he was searching for the right words to gently explain a bad situation. Looking directly at his wife, he said softly, "I'm afraid that I have some bad news."

Clayton had already thought out the scenario and envisioned their future. "I thought it was good news," he commented.

Two sets of hopeful eyes looked at the man from Coalman's Hill. The very man who'd saved them from another frozen winter. The one who had always assured that no one for miles and miles would ever be cold, hungry—or without a place to stay.

"God put this house here for everyone," he said in a methodical tone. "Now He's gone a step further and made this family even better."

Clara reached under the table to hold Walter's hand as they felt the presence of grace. Clayton's warm, loving face stared back as he continued. "Elizabeth has a new friend, who's also part mommy, and I've found my new fishin' buddy!" Raising his massive arms over the table, he opened his hands and said, "You two are just the Lord's way of answering our prayers. This place is no good if it's empty," he said, exchanging eye contact with the elder couple. "Just stay here with us and be family..."

Elizabeth left her chair and ran over to hug her *mommy*. A youthful Clara Rodman held the child. With tears running down her face, she looked up to the ceiling and beyond. The old woman wasn't so old anymore. She felt invigorated, knowing that she was being anointed by the family she'd always dreamed of...

The silence of deep appreciation and gratitude consumed the room, until Clayton spoke up. "Hey, I have an idea," he said. "Does anyone want to take a ride in the toboggan?"

For years, Clara and Walter had heard stories about riding down Coalman's Hill with Clayton Graves. Many described it as "The most fun I've had in my entire life!"

The child was coming out in Clara and Walter. "Can we?" they both asked with clenched fists and bulging eyes.

"You sure can!" answered Clayton. "Let Walter and I clean up after dinner while you girls get ready."

The famous toboggan once owned by the defunct coal company was perched at the crest of the hill. From stem to stern, its cargo consisted of a little girl wearing a pink stocking cap with matching mittens, a mammoth man looking like a clean-shaven black Santa Claus, and a giggly high school couple from yesterday.

Elizabeth was fully aware that this was the Rodmans' first ride down the hill. Like her papa, she also knew when to take control in order to assure safety for others. Her beautiful eyes had a twinkle in them as she gave a briefing. "We need to be safe," she explained. The couple paid close attention as she addressed the many possibilities of what could happen.

Anticipation started to build.

Each sat in their assigned positions, with the former halfback standing at the tail end. He understood to push the heavy sled on Elizabeth's cue and climb aboard. "It only takes a little push," said Clayton.

Peering over the curved shield were the careful eyes of Elizabeth Graves. The seven-year-old lookout took her job seriously, knowing that lives were dependent on her. She was made fully aware that this precautionary measure was the most important aspect of the ride. The young scout was determined to be flawless—just like her papa was when he led men into battle.

All was quiet as she looked from side to side, near and far—for anything that could endanger *her* cargo. After a long minute, she was relieved to find that the coast was clear. Elizabeth sat down and nestled between her grandfather's legs. With snow boots firmly planted on the floorboard and mittens grasping the edge of the wooden shield, she shouted her command: "We can go now!"

Everyone took a deep breath as Walter pushed the mighty sled. Immediately, it began its downhill decent with increasing speed. In one motion he hopped on board and took the remaining seat behind his wife.

The legendary ride was underway, with four screaming children having the time of their lives!

They approached the first turn with Clayton pulling on the rope and guiding them through. Gaining speed, the joyride straightened out, only to be challenged by the second curve. The exhilarating rush of speed, the brisk wind, and friends hanging on to one another for dear life was greatly intensified by the natural beauty they rode on. Shimmering crystals from the icy snow served as a red carpet for the path they traveled on. Entering the turn, they rode up high and soon glided back down as Clayton's strong hands positioned the runaway toboggan toward the open gate. They were now traveling at top speed as they gracefully swerved back and forth to avoid a few bumps.

Suddenly they found a missing gear when the waxed bottom rode over the frozen metal. This created an extra push for the astronauts, sending them through the open gates like a shot. What awaited next were the cushioning mounds of soft snow that guaranteed a safe stop.

Clayton saw a clearing that resembled a fluffy pillow. He steered toward it with the nose of the sled sending a spray of snow everywhere -as if they were in a water park. In seconds, the deeply powdered meadow brought the toboggan to rest in its tranquility.

The ride was over with hearts pounding and mouths wide open. All got out and looked around in amazement. The thrill they just experienced had momentarily left them speechless.

Looking above, they could see millions of glistening stars showing the path to Heaven. Soon their eyes followed the slalom they'd just traveled down until they were viewing the famous bunkhouse. Its age-old lights cast an almost golden glow that spread all directions. It seemed to be a *calling* that showed the newly-formed family their way back home.

Finally, Clara spoke first.

"Wow!"

Chapter VII

THE FOLLOWING MORNING FOUND Walter in the kitchen. He couldn't sleep because of a pressing situation that was becoming more and more prevalent: Clayton's health.

He'd noticed his friend's recent weight loss and the moments he appeared to be uncharacteristically frail. Sporadically, there were minor incidents that could have passed Clayton off as a harmless drunk. These occurrences were becoming more frequent and obvious to others. "Is Clayton feeling okay?" was the question his wife had asked the day before.

It was after their dash in the snow, when she'd watched the man she always regarded as invincible stumbling several times while out of breath. What was once a simple task that served as testimony to his strength, now seemed borderline impossible. When he and Walter tried dragging the heavy toboggan with its female cargo, the big man couldn't keep his end up. Clara instinctively got out to assist, with Elizabeth not being aware. "Don't worry about me," he said with a chuckle. "I'm just an old man getting his second wind."

Something was wrong, and it was time to take action. Walter would call Pastor Moore at daybreak and coordinate getting Clayton Graves to a doctor.

With the decision made, it was time to shift gears. The retired army cook got up early enough to have the entire kitchen to himself. Until that moment, it was others volunteering for kitchen duty with smiles on their faces. Now it was his turn—and Sergeant E-7 Walter Jeremiah Rodman had a few tricks up his sleeve...

Walter had no problems stocking the kitchen from the same commissary Clayton frequented. Food and other provisions were accessible to the point where they could easily supply any needy family in the area.

The former Connelly Award recipient looked at his watch and saw he had a good two hours to prepare a breakfast that would always be remembered.

His choice?

Walter's rendition of Eggs Benedict, with blueberry muffins and apple spice raisin oatmeal. A platter of maple-cured bacon, along with orange juice, hot cocoa, milk, and mountain fresh coffee would accompany this almost seven-course meal.

The combination of warm quilts and pleasant thoughts usually made one spend a little extra time in bed. This peacefulness, however, was boldly challenged by a succulent invitation coming from the kitchen.

Walter's cooking was further aided by a magnificent sunrise by our Creator. Together, they won out wholeheartedly. Immediately bathrobes, pajamas and slippers rounded the dining room table as Walter poured hot coffee and warm cocoa.

With a victorious grin, he raised his mug as the others followed suit and said, "Cheers!"

This moment was a page from another chapter of the house on Coalman's Hill. It seemed that anyone who ventured into the kitchen created a feast fit for kings. Throughout the meal, Elizabeth gazed at her father as he would take a bite of food and rest back in his chair. With eyes closed, he would raise his head and gently sway back and forth, savoring his breakfast. "Umm ummm," sighed Clayton. "We're living like royalty this morning!" he commented.

The little girl turned to watch the sun greet the day. To her delight, its florescent rays were stretched over another fresh blanket of snow. It was clear that the students in the surrounding area would be *forced* to miss more school.

Elizabeth tried to not to show her enthusiasm as she secretively clapped her hands under the table.

Walter saw something different at the table. The man he saw seemed to tremble a bit, and circles had formed under his eyes. Something was terribly wrong.

After breakfast, Walter excused himself to go outside. "I need some fresh air," he said. He put on his jacket and left through the front door, closing it behind him. When he had absolute privacy, he reached into his pocket and got out his cell phone. Immediately he dialed Pastor Moore's number to express his concern about Clayton's health.

"Myself and others have been concerned about Clayton," said the pastor. "He's lost a noticeable amount of weight and doesn't seem to be the man he used to be."

It was clear that Clayton needed to be transported to the hospital for a thorough evaluation—at once.

"I'll talk to Clara about this and get back to you within an hour," said Walter.

By 10:00 a.m. the stage was set. It was agreed that a hayride would gather the nearby families for a stay-over at church, one that could be extended for several days, if needed. The community would have enough musicians, adult supervision, and children to have non-stop activity. Outdoor bonfires, songs, sleigh rides, games, church services and inspiring sermons would be just a few of the events taking place at this spur-of-the-moment retreat. Most importantly, a sleigh would be waiting to take Clayton miles away to a four-wheel drive vehicle that would serve as the final relay to his destination: the Benson City Hospital.

For young Elizabeth, a different picture was painted. "He and his friends are just going out for a while," she would be told.

Clara took Elizabeth in front of the fireplace to crochet the afghan they had started. "We'll have fun while we do this and can talk about anything," she told the child. This was a ploy to give Walter the time needed to tactfully express the appointment he had made for his friend.

With determination, he gently tapped on Clayton's bedroom door. "Come in," came the soft response. Walter entered to find his friend sitting on the edge of his bed. He looked even wearier than he had at breakfast, prompting Walter to speak. He started off by saying how much everyone in the valley loved him. Without missing a beat, he pointed out all of the small mishaps occurring lately that seemed to illustrate a health problem.

"We decided to play it safe and scheduled an appointment for you," he said. "The hospital promised to examine you the moment you arrive." Staring directly at him, Walter continued.

"You just don't look like your usual self," he explained. "Myself and others are worried and beg you to do this for us."

Clayton was well aware that he was contending with some kind of ailment. He had lost his balance several times recently and would have spells of a feverish-dizzy feeling, where he would have to sit down.

The proud man always did the right thing, and this time was no different. Looking up to his friend, a tear trickled down his cheek. He felt good knowing that others cared about him so much. "I'll do if for everyone," he said, "and especially for Elizabeth."

Emotions took control as Walter bent over and hugged his friend with Clayton reciprocating.

Clayton got up and pulled his suitcase out of the closet. Walter left the bedroom and walked into the living room. His wife quietly noticed him as he gave a slight nod that telegraphed Clayton was being cooperative. The mother of the house suddenly acted excited and broke the good news to Elizabeth about having another stay-over at the church. "You'll have lots of friends there," she said.

Many calls had been made by Walter and Pastor Moore that morning. By the time Cider pulled in front of a house, its occupants were packed and ready to go. Soon they arrived in the church parking lot to see other sleighs full of caroling parishioners ready to have fun!

Off in the distant corner was an empty sleigh with a lone driver. His name was, Desmond Fields; a middle-aged African American deacon from a church miles away. The tall, lanky man knew Pastor Moore from the many conventions, church outings and services they'd shared through the years. Desmond traditionally wore a renowned smile that cast a spiritual glow from his soul. Birds were even known to land on his shoulders and chirp.

Today his facial expression was one of concern. He was summoned to secretively transport Clayton to a waiting all-terrain vehicle, hours away.

Chapter VIII

ELIZABETH GRAVES WAS A VERY popular young lady. This included her life at school, church, and beyond. She was always that honor student who sat in the front row of class, as well as all church sessions. The many sermons she'd heard made her feel *appointed* to get her school friends to attend church with her.

"It's a lot of fun," she would say. "There are so many things we do once we get there—and you make lots of friends."

The result?

A congregation that was full of her school friends! This included church activities that in time reached out to her school. Often, the young catalyst would recite a quote that she heard every Sunday. "We're all just one big family..."

Elizabeth got out of the sleigh and hugged her papa goodbye. She knew that he would be leaving to visit others who were far away. "I love you, Papa; hurry back!"

"I love you, too," he replied as he held her for a few precious seconds.

Immediately she grabbed her overnight bag and ran to the church's main doors. Once entering, her name was called out from all sides:

"Elizabeth!"

"Elizabeth, come over here!"

"Hey, girl!"

"Can I sit next to you at dinner?"

"I want to be on your team!"

Clara was touched by watching Elizabeth's reception. It was at that time when one of the greatest moments of her life took place. The child pointed at her and said, "Just as long as Clara is with us." Elizabeth then grabbed Clara's hand and gave a mighty tug, causing her to lose balance. The determined child would not let go and raced her over to a cluster of friends. "This is my friend, Clara," she announced. "She and her husband will be living with Papa and I for ever and ever!"

Overwhelmed and out of breath, she began to introduce herself to her new friends. It was understood that Clara would help Pastor Moore facilitate the many chores and activities that would take place. She was also just made aware that she was recruited by Elizabeth's peers—and would be doing double duty.

The old woman from the foothills of Coalman's Hill wouldn't have it any other way!

Pastor Moore was outside introducing Walter to Desmond. "Trust me," he assured while placing a hand on the deacon's shoulder. "Your friend, Clayton is in good hands."

"I know he is!" laughed Walter. Clayton's bag was in the sleigh with both men bundled up and secure on the bench seat. It was time to depart. Desmond shook the reins initiating his horse, Stardust, to begin the long trek.

Back inside, spaghetti was being prepared in the kitchen. Clara was delighted to find industrial-sized pots to serve the masses. While she was taking inventory on what the kitchen offered, she felt a tug on her dress. Turning around, she saw a familiar set of eyes with a beautiful smile. It was Elizabeth and her friends.

Her shiny teeth were all exposed when she announced, "We're here to help you!" It was just like being at home. Clara was being asked to teach them something, so that they could all do it together!

The girls proved to be very helpful. Not only did they set the tables in the dining room; they also helped served dinner. In fact, they wouldn't leave until everything was cleaned and put away.

Once finished, they surrounded Clara and paraded her up to their sleeping quarters. To her surprise, they'd made a bed for her and had it placed right smack-dab in the middle with Elizabeth. Pastor Moore was leaning against the door jamb, smiling with approval. Clara saw him and threw her hands up in the air, as if to say, "Well, what can I do?"

The pastor motioned her to join him as he turned around and left. In moments they were in his office. The good man couldn't stop staring at her. He saw how the girls chose to be with her and took the fight to her. Equally important; he noticed how good it made her feel.

"Clara loves children," Walter would say.

The pastor spoke. "We need women like you," he said. "This area has an abundance of children that either have mothers working long hours, or are from broken homes. I saw how much those girls love you. It's because you fill a void in their lives. You are that mom, big sister; friend they've been searching for."

In one motion Clara opened her mouth, placed her hand over her heart and learned back, speechless.

Pastor Moore continued. "Our church has programs for such needy children that cover this region. This includes Campfires, Girl Scouts, and many other youth services. Would you be interested in getting involved with making a difference in those very lives that need someone like you?" he asked.

Clara was flattered! All her life she wanted to do those very things rather than feeling that she'd gotten too old too fast and missed the boat.

Pastor Moore started to go into further detail. He did so by showing Clara brochures that had pictures of a happy elder woman taking kids camping, doing arts and crafts together and being there when they needed a hug.

Clara took the pamphlets and absorbed the smiles that each child had, smiles that came from a senior who also had a void to fill.

At that moment, she had a revelation.

It was no mistake that she and Walter were forced to move into the house on Coalman's Hill due to severe winter conditions.

She was the woman in those pictures.

The sleigh ride with Desmond was a taste of Heaven. It seemed that every time a fishing story, childhood story or milestone in life was told, a common name surfaced that the other knew from his past.

"Vernon Briggs?" asked Desmond in amazement. "Now how on Earth did you come to know him? That guy was my roommate every summer at camp!"

"You're kidding me!" said Clayton. "Mark Wesson and I played football together ever since grade school!"

"I don't believe it!" exclaimed Desmond. "My grandpa always talked about his childhood friend, Leroy Middleton. Why, they were practically brothers!"

Soon the journey's tempo took a foreseeable turn.

To the left in a clearing stood a series of gigantic iron rods that looked like strings to an icy harp. These noble poles formed a rectangle pattern that enclosed what looked like rows of uneven hedges, covered with snow. A closer look showed what appeared to be partially-hidden granite faces staring back, images that resembled Saint Nick peering underneath the furry outline of his cap, with his long, bushy beard ever present. One stone was slightly exposed more than the others. Etched across its front in bold print was the name GRAVES for all to see.

This was a sacred place for Clayton. It was a spiritual resting place set aside in the wilderness, where peace and tranquility reigned. It was where his family and many loved ones were laid to rest.

Desmond was all too familiar with this picturesque setting. As a deacon, he'd assisted many services which had processions that led there. Without saying a word, the kind man guided his horse to the cemetery's main entrance, where its majestic gates remained open.

Clayton was touched at his friend's thoughtfulness and looked at Desmond with a tear in his eye. "I truly appreciate this," he said. Desmond tipped his hat out of respect, and the mountain man nodded back. Stardust had come to a stop, and Clayton climbed out of the sleigh. "This shouldn't be too long," he said.

"Take your time," came Desmond's reply. "We're in no hurry..."

The abundance of fallen snow didn't hinder Clayton from knowing where each loved one resided. Crystallized flakes crunched under his feet as he walked forward.

A pleasant surprise awaited.

There before him was the resting place of his childhood friend, Lamar Smith. Next to his marker was a beautiful cardinal, obviously looking for food. The element of God-given life brought a huge smile to Clayton's face as he stopped and leaned over. In a soft, high-pitched voice he asked, "Did you make a friend today, Lamar?" Reaching into his pocket, he grabbed a small handful of birdseed. With caution he gently tossed it toward the snow-covered monument and stepped back.

Out of nowhere came many birds gliding in to eat the seeds. "Well!" said Clayton. "It looks like you brought your friends with you. That's okay, though," he added. "Everyone is always welcome here." He reached into his pocket, grabbed a generous helping of seed and gave it an underhanded toss in the general area. Many chirping sounds filled the lot as Clayton responded. "That's okay," he said in a joyous tone. "It's just a gift from my friends and I, thanking you for dropping by."

His visit continued as he trudged through the deep snow, acknowledging other friends and relatives. Finally he stood in front of his wife, daughter, mom and dad. With sincere concentration he bowed his head and prayed. Once finished, he raised his head and said, "As you all know, I'm going to see a doctor. Please pray for me, because Elizabeth will always need me."

Tears returned to his face.

Clayton was fully aware that he could be leaving this world soon—leaving the sole survivor of the family line behind. He was in deep thought and bowed once again to pray further. Eventually he finished, raised his head and parted. It was time to return to the sleigh and continue their journey.

The two men were once again traveling down the country road that connected the hills with the city. Gradually, it began to get dark as more snow fell, with Stardust maintaining a brisk pace. The men didn't mind at all. They were having too much fun sharing the many adventures they had growing up. Soon they were on a long stretch of flatland when the lights of a Bronco flashed them. "That's my son," said Desmond. "He's a wonderful boy and will get you safely to the hospital."

This was a special moment in Clayton's life. It was a Godsend to have a man like Desmond in his life, especially under the circumstances given. "I am so happy to know you, Desmond," said Clayton. "I can't express how grateful I am being able to meet your son."

It was also a special moment for Desmond as he commented, "It's our pleasure."

Stardust came to a stop next to the vehicle with studded tires. The men got out of the sleigh to stretch their legs. At that time, the driver opened the door and anxiously walked up to Clayton. The thirty-year-old man was an imposing force to be reckoned with. He was much bigger than his father and had monstrous-sized hands. He towered over the two seniors. Clayton was at a loss for words—until the son's warm demeanor was exposed. He was blessed with the family trait of his father's smile.

"Clayton," said Desmond. "This is my son, Jason. I promise that he will get you to the front steps of the hospital with no problem."

The loyal son introduced himself by extending his hand toward Clayton. "You must be Clayton Graves," he said in a friendly tone. "There have been many wonderful things said about you in these parts."

"I can see your father in you," said Clayton.

Jason got a little bashful and laughed while looking at his dad. "That's what I like to hear," he said.

There was a brief visit amongst the three men, with laughter and handshakes bringing it to a close. "Are you going to be okay?" Clayton asked Desmond. "I hate to leave you here."

"You're not leaving me stranded," he replied. Pointing at a snow-covered lane that went between some trees, he said, "My wife and I live just beyond there. She has a warm meal waiting for me—so I'll be just fine. What I want is to hear good reports from the hospital," he said.

"I'll do my best," promised Clayton.

It was time for the journey to continue. Jason addressed his dad, saying, "Tell mom I say hi, and let me know if you need me for anything."

"Okay, son," answered his dad. Desmond climbed up on the bench of his sleigh, and with a gentle pull, guided Stardust home.

The Ford's cushioned seats and heating system had Clayton in the lap of luxury. Its smooth ride over the packed ice gave a massaging effect that made staying awake almost impossible. It was Jason's conversation and quick wit that kept him alert and interested.

The barren road of frozen tundra gradually became pavement, and houses became more prevalent. Soon a red octagon sign stood in defiance, commanding them to stop. Once it was verified that the intersection was safe to cross, Jason proceeded by taking a sharp right turn. In minutes they found themselves on a city street laced with streetlights and neon signs. Wide avenues with noisy traffic and litter held the community at ransom.

The contrast between being in God's country to being in a congested population that never coordinated anything with the sunrise was rude, to say the least. After several major intersections and a few irresponsible drivers, a gargantuan structure came into view. "That's where we're going," pointed out Jason. The hospital was further away than it appeared as they drove toward it. Finally they arrived, and in the blink of an eye were fortunate enough to park in a stall that was only a few feet away from the main entrance.

This was the Benson City Hospital, and it was one of the nation's most modern facilities. Dr. Schoenberg had comforted Pastor Moore over the phone by emphasizing, "We have the technology to find what's ailing Clayton."

Chapter IX

JASON'S HOSPITALITY HAD only begun. He carried Clayton's suitcase into the hospital and made sure he was properly admitted. The receptionist had been foretold about Clayton Graves. Her orders were to have the necessary paperwork filled out and have the patient wait in the lobby while notifying Dr. Schoenberg.

Once the formalities were done, the men sat in an open area that contained beautiful leather furniture, a matching coffee table, and ferns that enhanced the waiting area like an oasis. Jason's humanity continued. He ensured with compassion that everything that could be done, would be.

At that moment the figure of a stout middle-aged man entered the lobby. Wavy silver hair and wire-rimmed glasses personified a look that exemplified he was a product of higher education. A white medical outfit with a pager fastened to his belt went beyond suspicion and clearly showed that he was of great importance. He stood still while scanning the room with a look of urgency.

He noticed the two men who were engaged in a friendly conversation, and a smile slowly came across his face. He walked toward the gathering with assurance and approached what had to be 'The Mountain Man Of Coalman's Hill.' "Clayton Graves?" asked the prestigious doctor.

The two looked over and saw the dignified man.

"You must be Dr. Schoenberg, that 'whiz-bang doctor' Pastor Moore speaks so highly of," responded Clayton.

"Well, I guess that's who I am," laughed the surgeon in a gracious tone. He then extended his hand and gave Clayton a firm handshake, one that created a bond.

He took a seat and momentarily gazed at the man who sat before him. Dr. Schoenberg had heard stories about Clayton Graves. Numerous times, the name was mentioned when a patient reminisced about surviving frigid winters on Coalman's Hill. The good doctor felt honored having met this real-life folk hero.

Looking at the weakened man, he could see the darkened eyes, apparent loss of weight, and a slight trembling. Immediately his professional eye took an educated guess on what these symptoms suggested. All at once, a gut feeling came across him that made him feel sick inside.

Dr. Johann Michael Schoenberg hoped that his hindsight would be proven wrong. Regardless, if he *was* facing a dying man, he would do everything within his capacity to save him. Dr. Schoenberg held a poker face and spoke with his mild accent.

"You've traveled far to get here, Mr. Graves," said the doctor.

"Call me Clayton," he said with a wink. "That's what everyone calls me."

That comment gave the foreign-born surgeon a warm feeling. *He really is everyone's friend,* Johann Michael Schoenberg thought to himself.

It was now time to discuss business. "Arrangements have been made to keep you here as long as necessary to find out what's wrong with you," said Dr. Schoenberg. "You might be released as early as tomorrow sometime, or it could take much longer. We won't know until we run tests to conclude what we're up against."

Clayton understood the information and nodded quietly.

There was more conversation between doctor and patient. After a few minutes the tempo had changed to an open discussion that ranged from sports to vacation spots.

Bedtime found Clayton alone in his room. His stomach was pleasantly full after enjoying a dinner in the hospital cafeteria with Dr. Schoenberg and Jason. He was now in a plush room with floral accents and wood trim. To his right was a breathtaking view from the tenth floor that overlooked a harbor. In front of him was a color television set suspended from the ceiling with its remote within arm's reach. A few tasteful paintings graced the walls to balance out the room. He was indeed being catered to as if he was royalty, and in the best room he'd ever stayed in (away from home).

This was the calm before the storm.

His schedule for the following day would be a busy one. He was to be wheeled around from one floor to another, taking one test after another with meals in between.

Despite the fear of the unknown, all he could think about was Elizabeth. He was worn out from the long day and turned out the light. The man from Coalman's Hill would now say his goodnight prayers—including a special little prayer sent for a special little girl...

Chapter X

CLARA RODMAN STOOD IN the kitchen, stirring a pot of hot oatmeal. Brown sugar, milk, and an array of fruit would feed the troops after Pastor Moore's blessings.

Like a few select adults, she was preoccupied in thought over Clayton's welfare. Rumors were starting to spread that he was stricken with a terminal disease and given little time. "Oh, don't be silly," she would say. "He's just gone off with his friends and will be back here before you know it."

A fair answer coming from a loved one who didn't actually know...

Clara was up early, as she was every morning with plenty on her mind. Stirring the oatmeal cereal with a large wooden spoon, she pondered the fate of her dear friend Clayton Graves as her husband stood next to her.

Walter was also a 'morning person' who traditionally handled such matters in a calm fashion. This time it was different. A look of depression was occasionally seen on his face. Despite having many friends who had passed through the years, this situation was different. This was his friend, Clayton; the man who took him and his wife in. the one who gave them a family—and changed their lives forever.

It was the crack of dawn, and the married couple was looking out the kitchen window. There they saw a slight haze outlining the surrounding mountains. Pastel violets and reds painted a sky that extended over miles and miles of snowy hills. This was how they knew life and the people they loved. They always started off their day together watching the sunrise, rain or shine.

In silence, each was saying a prayer for Clayton.

At that moment they slowly turned around, only to be startled by a cluster of smiling faces staring back. Arms and shoulders involuntarily rolled in a backward motion as toes briefly elevated, with every muscle in their faces tightening. Their hearts nearly skipped a beat as the little voices yelled, "Surprise!"

It was none other than Elizabeth Graves herself, leading the pack and delivering a message. "We're going to help you with breakfast!"

The unity that was established the day before was now reaching new heights. Clara was definitely *in* with this group, and could only bend over with open arms to initiate a massive group hug.

Walter loved what he saw. It was the mother coming alive in his wife. He left the room, so as not to interfere.

In Benson City, Clayton Graves had a visitor in his room: Jason Fields. He was dressed and sitting with him at a table.

"Did you sleep good last night?" asked Jason.

"I slept fine, but still wish I was back home," answered Clayton.

"I bet you miss that wonderful grandchild of yours," said Jason. "My dad says that she's a gem!"

Clayton was just getting ready to call Walter when Jason showed up. Walter knew that Clayton's contact was meant for Elizabeth and would get her promptly. "Would you like to speak to her?" he asked Jason with a glow on his face.

"I'd love to!" he exclaimed.

With phone in hand, Clayton dialed. In a moment it was picked up on the other end with Clayton saying, "Good morning, Walter; you know what to do."

It didn't take long for Clayton's ears to perk up. He became ecstatic, like a child on Christmas morning, as he grabbed the phone with both hands. He addressed his granddaughter with his natural, jubilant voice. "Is this my little Elizabeth?"

"Papa, I miss you!" she replied with excitement.

It was heartwarming for Jason to watch the inner spirit of Clayton Graves come alive. Like everyone else, he knew that nothing made him happier than his 'little angel', Elizabeth.

The bantering of exchanging adventures went back and forth, with Clayton's face expressing joy from every tidbit Elizabeth shared.

"I bet they're all happy that you are there with them," he commented.

"You did, did you?" he would inject.

"That's why everyone loves you so much," he would add. "And I love you too!"

The call was brief as her papa gave her peace of mind. "Don't listen to those silly rumors," he said. "I'll be home real soon, and we'll show 'em! Don't worry about me. I'm doing just fine over here, but I do miss you so very much... I'll be back home in a day or two," he said with conviction. "And hey, there's someone here who wants to speak to you."

The phone was handed to Jason, who asked, "Is this Elizabeth?"

A brief conversation took place, with Jason introducing himself and exchanging sweet for sweet. The new acquaintances volleyed back and forth for a few minutes, until Jason said, "Okay, and I feel the same... Here's your papa. Bye, Elizabeth!" Jason handed the phone back to Clayton and gave him a thumbs-up.

Clayton took the phone and conversed a bit more. Then he finished off with, "Bye, darling. I love you!"

Clayton waited until he heard the words needed to help him survive the day: "Bye, Papa. I love you too."

After the call, Clayton felt richer and addressed his friend. "Dr. Schoenberg visited me this morning. He told me to have breakfast, then meet him here at eight o'clock. He said we were going to have a long day that would include blood tests, X-rays, ultrasounds, and other things. It'll be the kind of day where I wouldn't be good for any company once it's over." He stared at the attentive face that was listening and elaborated further. "I was told that if all went well, I'd be released tomorrow morning and then hear from them within a few days."

All was quiet until Jason spoke up. "I guess that we can have one last meal together, and then your doctor can call me when it's time for me to take you home."

"That sounds about right," replied Clayton.

Jason turned his head and noticed a clock on the wall. It showed that they had forty-five minutes until Clayton's procedures were to take place. Without any words being spoken, the two headed out to the cafeteria. A hearty breakfast was about to take place, with thanks given. Pleasant conversation with words of encouragement would be included.

The satisfying meal came to an end at almost the top of the hour with parting handshakes turning into hugs. "Good luck, Clayton. I'll be here for you," promised Jason.

The grateful man placed his hand on the young man's shoulder and said, "I know you will."

Clayton's day had him wearing a hospital gown that exposed his backside. It started off with a routine physical that included an interview about his medical history and family background. From there he was escorted into some rooms, and wheeled into others. Sometimes he sat up straight to allow blood to be drawn; other times he had to lay down in a specific pose and hold still.

A mundane, nutritious lunch divided his day, with more tests to follow. Finally, he was resting in his assigned bed with a dinner tray suspended over his lap. The mountain man was fatigued. He ate his meal, and moments later drifted off to sleep.

The next morning consisted of a meeting with Dr. Schoenberg in his room. He was satisfied with what was accomplished the day before and said, "Now we have what's needed to pinpoint our problem."

The business-like tempo changed as the briefing transpired into a visit that implied a warm friendship. Dr. Schoenberg had taken off his glasses and was now acting like Johann Michael Schoenberg: an interesting man with a unique background. Some laughter along with a few amazing stories rotated back and forth, until a professional handshake was given to finalize their first round.

"You can go home now," he said, gently patting Clayton on his shoulder. "You'll be hearing from me within a few days," he said. "It's been a pleasure meeting you, Clayton. Please feel free to contact me if you have any questions." The caring physician put his glasses back on and looked at his clipboard. He then stood up and left the room to continue his busy schedule.

Later, Jason met Clayton in the lobby to take him home. "Any news?" he asked.

"He'll get in touch with me in a few days," came Clayton's reply.

Jason took charge of his leg of the relay. With Clayton dressed and ready to go, he carried the elder's luggage to his vehicle and drove them to his father's waiting sleigh. "It's been great meeting you," expressed Jason with sincerity. "Drop by and visit us whenever you're in town."

Warm goodbyes took place, and a bond for life had been established. The Graves family now extended to the city of Benson. Clayton was beyond grateful for what Jason had done for him. It was now time to leave son for father, and drift back into the countryside where he belonged. Desmond and Stardust were ready and well-prepared. Roast beef sandwiches, along with fruit, cookies, and mugs of hot cider would make a picnic out of this sleigh ride.

"How was your stay?" asked the chauffeur with the loving smile.

"Everyone was just great to me," said Clayton as he placed his suitcase in the back of the sleigh. "You certainly have a wonderful boy," he added.

"Why, thank you," replied the deacon in his happy tone. Clayton climbed up onto the buckboard and sat next to him. Once seated, gloved hands gave a slight jiggle on the reins, giving Stardust its signal to march forward.

Immediately, hoofed steps kicked up fluffy snow as the sleigh jerked into a sliding rhythm. It was now the best part of the journey: returning home with time not being a factor. More importantly, it was a brotherhood between the two God-fearing men—one that shared more stories and delicious food while giving praise to the Lord.

Ahead lay peaceful miles of a snow-covered back road, a heavenly path that led to an enchanted cemetery, Pastor Moore's church, and the legendary bunkhouse on Coalman's Hill...

Chapter XI

CLAYTON GRAVES HAD BEEN HOME for two days when his phone rang. It was his newly formed friend, Dr. Schoenberg, with a sense of urgency in his voice. "We need you to get here at once to perform more tests," he said.

His conversation was brief and to the point. "I have received the results from the tests we did recently, and they don't look good. I want to check further before I form a conclusion."

The good doctor had been in contact with Pastor Moore, who in turn had coordinated a second trip with Desmond Fields and his son, Jason. It was already prearranged to have Desmond pick him up in his sleigh that afternoon.

"I'll get ready," came Clayton's quiet response.

The most recent church function included all of the families in the area. This let Clayton know that for the next few days, all were taken care of. He discussed the phone call with Walter and said, "It's best that you stay here and take care of Elizabeth and Clara. Desmond and I will be fine."

The brave commander had lots on his mind as he went to his room to pack his suitcase. Alone, he was deep in thought, taking inventory of himself. He was aware that he was still losing weight and his strength was slipping. He also knew that his physical changes were making others concerned. Dr. Schoenberg's phone call was more of a wake-up call. He was now getting mentally prepared to face the most important challenge of his life—*if that's what it was.*

When he finished packing, he turned around and caught himself staring back in the mirror. What he saw was a grim reality. It was an old man, slightly hunched over and wearing baggy clothes; a man who had seen better days. A closer look showed a weathered face that was starting to sag. Even worse, there was no smile. Clayton waved at the reflection, which waved back. There was no mistaking who that man was.

Clayton Graves loved life. His phone call with Dr. Schoenberg reminded him of how precious it really was, and made him ponder *why* he was really 'here'. The mountain man thought about his neighbors who relied on him—not just during a hard winter, but year round. He then thought about all of his friends from church and other social outlets. People he camped, fished, and worshiped with.

People he felt a *calling* to be there for.

Drifting back into the archives of his mind, he recalled the many times he was fortunate enough to help a stranger in need. Jumper cables, an extra can of gasoline, and leaving a crate of food on the front steps for a struggling family when nobody was home were some of the memories that surfaced. Then there was the time when he used an inflatable raft to save a boy in Coalman's Creek—a boy who went on to become a self-sacrificing youth counselor throughout the county.

Those people will never know how honored I was to be there for them, he thought to himself.

He began to think about his dwindling family and the many friends that had passed one by one to be with the Lord. Their lives had given him yet another reason to live life to its fullest and care for others.

At that moment his thoughts became distracted, as if something pressing needed to be addressed *right now*. It was a distinct feeling, an aura that seemed to take control. It was as if he was being commanded to look around and find what was patiently waiting for his attention.

Clayton never questioned a feeling that came from within. He cautiously looked around the room. While moving slightly back and forth, he swayed his head from side to side, up and down, knowing that *something* was there for him.

It wasn't until he saw the picture displayed on his nightstand that it hit him like a ton of bricks. Staring directly at him was an intense set of loving eyes penetrating his soul. It was his favorite picture of Elizabeth. Together they were posed on a hay ride, wearing straw hats with matching flannel shirts that were partially covered with golden hay, along with glowing, radiant smiles. Like every day of their life, this too was one of their happiest moments.

Seeing his little angel always removed any stress or anxiety that he might have been feeling on a given day. Immediately, her innocent smile brought him back to his senses and allowed him to laugh at himself.

It was now time to take an extended walk down Memory Lane a little further...

He remembered the night when a lightning storm with booming thunder scared her. The frightened child ran into his room and jumped on his bed, hugging him with both arms. "It's just lightning," he said in a comforting tone. "That's just the Lord putting on a light show for us to enjoy the rain." Papa also had an explanation for the shaking thunder from the sky. "That's just part of their music up there," he would say. "They have the best parties up there, but sometimes they get a little carried away, playing their music loud enough for the whole universe to hear..."

It became their house policy that whenever our Creator had a light show with loud booming, she was allowed to go into her papa's room and hug him—without even knocking. They would simply watch the show together!

Every day he marveled at the beautiful works of art she created that spread her happiness. Watercolors, paintings, hand prints and sculptures that were all expressed with her little touch.

He thought of the many times she hugged him, whether she was happy or afraid, the moments when she needed him, knowing that he would always be there, and the emotional needs that always brought tears to his eyes and made him a stronger man.

It then occurred to him that Elizabeth was the final ingredient that put everything into perspective. It was his seven-year-old granddaughter who gave him his greatest reason for wanting to be alive.

For the first time in Clayton Grave's life, he feared death.

He sat on the edge of his bed in an attempt to muster up what strength he had. Leaning forward with hands pressed against his face, he started to gather himself. The aging man knew that he had to face this uncertainty head-on. He was also aware that he needed to create a little quality time for Elizabeth, a special little one-on-one where he would tactfully explain to her the best he could about having to leave again.

Questions like 'Where are you going?' and 'Are you okay?' were inevitable.

The dedicated grandfather didn't want to alarm her unnecessarily, but he didn't want to lie either. Clayton looked at the clock on the wall and realized that it was just a matter of time until Desmond arrived.

Dressed and ready to go, he left his bedroom to place his suitcase by the front door. Next in order was to find Elizabeth and have their sit-down. Before he could find her, she found him.

"Where are you going, Papa?" she asked, wrapping her arms around his waist.

"So there you are," he responded, wrapping his arms around her and swaying side to side.

"How's my little angel today?" he asked.

"Fine," she said with a sniffling sound.

Clayton extended his arms to expose Elizabeth's face. What he saw was a teary-eyed child that almost made *him* cry. "Are you crying?" he asked with a concerned expression.

The little girl broke into tears and buried her face into his stomach. "Are you sick, Papa?" she cried out.

It was a moment of truth. "Well, yes I am, kinda," he said. "That's why I went to see a doctor. It's always a good idea to see a doctor if you're not sure if you're feeling well," he explained, patting her on the back.

That answer registered with Elizabeth. Her trembling body and sniffling nose began to subside as she leaned back and looked at him. "You mean you're going to be all right?" she asked with a sound of hope in her voice.

"I think so," he answered with his usual jovial pitch. Then his facial expression turned into one of confidence. Leaning close to one ear, he said with conviction, "If I can protect this country

64

without ever losing a man, what makes you think that I can't beat this little thing?"

A look of relief gradually came over his granddaughter's face. Looking at the man she loved, Elizabeth said, "Nothing can stop you!"

The former commander placed his hands on her shoulders. He leaned within inches of her face and calmly said, "That's right, my little darling. Nothing!"

He then stepped back, stood straight at attention and saluted his little soldier. Having been properly trained, Elizabeth got into a perfect stance and saluted back. Then they lunged at each other and embraced in a bear hug. Clayton was momentarily the big man he always was. He picked her up with ease and carried her over to the dining room table.

The stage was set perfectly.

The beloved Clayton Graves was sitting at the table, with Elizabeth already feeling much better. Using a thick British accent, he spoke:

"Shall we have some tea, my dear?"

Elizabeth laughed and without hesitation got out of her chair to make a pot of tea. Long ago, her papa taught her how to make tea—as long as he was present. Clara and Walter were watching from the door jamb and loved what they saw. They always admired how Clayton could make anyone laugh, regardless of the situation. They also understood the importance of this moment and left quietly.

The little girl in pajamas carefully filled the tea pot with water and placed it on the stove. She then turned the dial that would cause the water to boil. Next, she went to the china closet and brought back two tea cups with matching saucers. Clayton remained still as the little girl got two teabags for two people and placed one in each cup.

Within five minutes, tea was served, as Clayton's antics continued. He took his large hands and delicately used his index finger and thumb to pick up the hot cup, with his pinky pointing straight out. Sipping the tea, he incorporated a smug expression as he slightly smacked his lips like a prudish old queen. Maintaining the same accent, he spoke in a high-pitched, graceful tone:

"Oh, I do say, my dear, this is quite lovely..."

Elizabeth couldn't hold in her laughter anymore and broke out into hysterics. Clayton placed his cup down and howled with a heartiness that shook the table. The tempo had become one of happiness as Clayton addressed the real topic.

"You don't need to get sad when I'm under the weather," he said. "It's like the times when you got sick and I took care of you. If there is something bad with me, I know that you'll take care of me—and then I'll get better."

It all made sense to Elizabeth, and she nodded her head. "It's just that people started asking me if you were sick," she said.

Papa leaned forward and said gently, "That's because around here, everyone looks out for one another. And they're right," he added, raising his hands. "I have been a little sick lately," he admitted. "Some of our friends could tell and simply wanted me to see a doctor; that's all."

The conversation continued. "Today I'm going to see the doctor again, just to make sure I'm getting better. And you know what?" he asked.

Elizabeth was starting to get enthused and shook her smiling face side to side.

"I just made a new friend because of this!" proclaimed her papa. "His name is, Desmond, and he serves in a church just down the mountain. He's a wonderful man who has some of the same friends I do."

Elizabeth's eyes lit up, illustrating that she wanted to hear more.

"See what the Lord does for us? He is always putting good people in our life," explained her papa. "We had a lot of fun the past few days, didn't we?" he asked.

Elizabeth was now wearing an ear-to-ear grin with all of her teeth showing as she nodded her head in agreement.

With gusto, Papa answered his own question. "That's because we always have fun—and God wouldn't want it to be any other way!"

That did it!

The little girl was cured of any worries and left her chair to give her hero a big hug, saying, "I love you, Papa."

"I love you too," he replied, rubbing her back.

Suddenly a voice entered the room. "Well, that must be your wonderful granddaughter I've heard so much about."

Clayton and Elizabeth turned around to see the compassionate face of one Desmond Miller Fields. The good man might have been new to Elizabeth's life, but he was no stranger to the house on Coalman's Hill. Years ago, his parents told countless stories about the famous Graves family and the wonderful things they'd done for others. Then the day came when his uncle took him up to the 'old coal mine' to look around.

The coal may have been extracted from the ground years ago, but its bunkhouse still breathed life. And now, he finally got to enter it for the first time. Looking around the room that was built at the turn of the century, his eyes were wide open in awe. "So this is the place that everyone has been talking about," he said under his breath.

Clayton looked at his new friend and said, "Desmond, it's so good to see you!"

Desmond broke out of his trace. His smile returned as he approached Clayton with hand extended. Shaking his friend's hand while patting his back, he asked, "And how's my friend feeling today?"

"Feeling just fine," came the reply as he winked at Elizabeth.

The little girl smiled back with reassurance.

"Well, good!" exclaimed Desmond.

The lean man with a bald head turned to Elizabeth. Bending over, he further displayed his charm. "Good morning, Elizabeth. My name is, Desmond and it's a pleasure to meet you."

Elizabeth fidgeted as she said, "My name is Elizabeth Graves and it's a pleasure to meet you."

Desmond was taken by her politeness. "Why, thank you, Elizabeth. I have heard many wonderful things about you."

Clayton knew why Desmond was there and addressed business. "I have my suitcase packed and I'm ready to go."

"Okay," replied Desmond. "I guess the sooner we leave, the sooner we get back."

"That's right," agreed Clayton.

Elizabeth ran out of her chair and wrapped her arms around her papa. "Please hurry back, Papa."

Clayton held the child and said, "We'll get back home as fast as we can."

The visit moved to the living room in front of the fireplace. Clara had already been introduced to Desmond and was busy in the kitchen. Using TV trays in front of a freshly stoked fire, the men were served a warm meal. She also packed a lunch that included a thermos full of hot chicken noodle soup and one of coffee for the long, frozen road that awaited them.

Clayton and Desmond were now bundled up in the sleigh. Walter, along with Elizabeth and Clara, stood on the front steps saying their goodbyes. "I love you, Papa," called out Elizabeth. "Get better and hurry back home!" she added.

"Be careful," said Clara.

"You guys have fun!" yelled Walter.

Desmond pointed at the little girl waving on the steps. "Your grandaddy is going to be just fine," he said.

"Don't worry about us," injected Clayton with a reassuring voice. "We're just a couple of guys going for a sleigh ride!"

Desmond shook the reigns and Stardust took its initial steps. The sleigh became more distant as it started to blend in with the mild flurry that surrounded it. Soon it became a part of the snowfield it was traveling in and disappeared.

Chapter XII

ELIZABETH KEPT WATCHING until her papa was no longer in sight, until the sounds of hoofs and friendly bantering could no longer be heard. Alone and in silence, she said a prayer and went inside.

Elizabeth took off her coat and draped it on the coat rack. Turning around, she saw Clara smiling at her and holding two sets of crocheting needles. Their afternoon was obviously planned. The mother figure had their afghan project spread out in front of the fireplace, with an array of colorful yarn at their disposal.

Walter liked what he saw. The dedicated husband always felt that he had failed his wife by never having children of their own—until they took up residence with the Graves family. The man saw that the women would spend the rest of the afternoon having their much-needed 'quality time' and left undetected.

It was now his turn—and nature was calling. Walter would dress warm, go out to the shed where he stored his snowshoes and put them on. Always one to be prepared, he would bring a compass, a bag full of bread scraps, peanuts, and a small pail. *Maybe I'll run into a pack of hungry deer, or find some winter berries to pick,* he thought to himself.

There was something about that day that had one Walter Rodman bring an extra precautionary measure, just in case. It was a vintage survival pack that his father always brought whenever they hiked, one that was regarded as a family heirloom. It was an antique canvas purse-like container with a long strap that fitted over one shoulder. Engraved on the brown leather strap was the name *Francis Grover Rodman.* In it was a tiny metal stand that held a tin cup over a small candle. There was also a knife, spoon, fork, matches, paper, a few granola bars, and pouches of instant cider and chicken broth. An extra pair of gloves, along with a ski mask and neck scarf, was neatly placed off to one side.

With tennis-racket-like shoes strapped to his boots, he high-stepped into the Arctic environment and toward a snowdrift. Walter was in his element. The country boy in him was alive, and the spirit of the wilderness beckoned him. He would now partake in the tranquility of God's crystal world. This Heavenly wonderland was only meant for the inhabitants who lived there and the few souls that would regard it as sacred.

The former Scout leader recalled the many times he ventured into the woods to take youth groups out for their first camp out. The outings focused on picking up litter, feeding deer, and sharing a group prayer at the campfire. Fond memories spawned from his early childhood, whenever his father took him out for a few days to live in God's world.

A soft breeze whispered through the surrounding bare branches as graceful glitters of flakes danced everywhere he looked, making the man feel accepted. To Walter, it was our Creator welcoming him.

His journey continued.

Carefully placing his feet one in front of the other, he came across a stream that was not entirely frozen. To his delight, a family of deer stood on the opposite bank, taking a drink. His nature skills made him fully aware that the small herd knew of his presence for some time. Still, it was understood that he was harmless, and possibly considered one of them.

Walter reached for the bag and grabbed a generous handful of bread scraps. In one smooth motion, he threw the bread within a few feet of the herd. Sparrows immediately glided in as the hiker threw another handful.

This was how he understood life:

It was the harmony of everything ever created, surviving together without a ripple.

The man who hated to wear a watch and rose with every sunrise watched in solitude. What he saw was how simple life was meant to be. How perfect it was within itself.

Walter had a passing thought about his friend, Clayton Graves, and the similarities they shared. One in-particular came to mind: Each always took the extra measure to feed any needy family they might happen across.

The creek flowed between cliffs, ridges and boulders, running parallel with a tree line. This natural pairing would serve Walter like a road map etched in stone. He would simply play it safe and use it as a guide line that would make his return trip uncomplicated.

Half an hour passed. Walter observed steep cliffs, frozen waterfalls, and icicles scattered about. On occasion, a furry winter coat would scamper home with nuts in its cheek.

The sixty-five-year-old man was ever-alert whenever he hiked in the woods during the winter months. He was especially cautious when alone. Still, there was something inside him that *wanted* to venture a bit further.

He hiked past a few more trees and around a bend. All at once something took him by surprise. The slight snow flurry that had been pulsating off and on had subsided briefly, leaving the sky still. It was there he saw something that caused reason for alarm. It was a thin stream of smoke reaching into the cold sky that could only be a campfire. A campfire out in the middle of a *frozen nowhere*.

There was something wrong with this picture, and it was time to investigate. Walter was in excellent condition for a man his age. He picked up his pace and made a beeline to see what he might find. With determination, he marched toward what he feared to be a distress signal. Closing in, he saw a cluster of trees about fifty yards away. Within its tight formation was a withering strand of smoke that was almost diminished. Seeing an opening between the trees, he charged forward and soon broke through. At that moment Walter saw *why* he was brought there.

There before him was a huddled group of campers, shivering around a dying fire. Next to them stood a florescent orange pole. It rose five feet above the frozen ground and proudly waved a triangular flag with the number 142 on it. It was like a scene out of Jack London's *To Build A Fire,* with Troop Number 142 at the mercy of the unforgiving temperatures.

Chapter XIII

SOMETHING COMPELLED WALTER RODMAN to venture outside that day, and specifically in that direction. It was the same funny feeling he had when he and Clayton agreed that he was needed to stay behind and watch over things.

Walter always knew to follow anything he interpreted as a premonition. Anytime he got itchy feet and felt a calling to go into the wilderness, he went without question. *Our Lord always has something waiting for me out here,* he would remind himself.

This particular hike would be more of a pilgrimage to find out *why* he felt the need to go.

Initially it started off as a simple day hike in the snow...

Grateful friends dressed in fur, feathers and antlers were waiting for Walter to feed them. There were also rock formations layered with silver and blue ice formations. Often, the stillness of a small waterfall that had its flow crystallized into silence would come into view. Within it drooped suspended icicles that varied in shapes and sizes, casting shadows. Images were formed, with some appearing to be the mystical face of Old Man Winter himself. Comforting faces that seemed to say, *Welcome to my world!*

This stronghold of nature was beyond any fairy tale, however. It was just another dimension of God's kingdom—the time of year when He turned back the clock to the serenity of creation. This seasonal winter world of untouched snow fields and peacefulness was much more than a sanctuary.

It was a restricted haven, meant only for those who lived there—and the chosen few who were invited.

Walter's gut feeling to go outside and follow his instincts had served him correctly. It was an impulse that registered so deeply that he brought along his father's personal survival kit. He also felt an inclination to follow a specific path seldom hiked during the snow season. It was a mission meant for the area's most experienced snowbound hiker with survival skills.

This was undoubtedly a calling, a spiritual walk that would guide him to Scouting Troop Number 142.

Walter had been summoned for a rescue mission.

His fists turned white as his heart pumped fast. Throughout his life he'd read about such incidents that resulted in tragedy. *If only I was there to help* he would say in prayer. Such a prayer was answered that day—and Walter Rodman knew what to do.

The seven shivering bodies told the story with bare hands almost touching the flame. Their bright nylon snow gear had already surrendered to the piercing chill. A closer look showed that a black book was being passed around from person to person. It was apparent that all were taking turns reading excerpts out loud.

Swiftly, he took long strides that drew attention. A lowered head that faced him looked up and began to wave frantically. Icy woolen ski hats turned and saw Walter Rodman. Without hesitation, the seasoned hiker projected a voice of authority. "Don't worry; everything will be just fine."

Immediately, the scared faces cast smiles of *knowing.* Shivering bodies that refused to give up hope now had reason to rejoice.

Their prayer had been answered.

Walter's mere presence held everyone's attention as he stood amongst the stranded hikers. He inauspiciously assessed the situation while calmly introducing himself. "My name is Walter Rodman," he said in a comforting tone as he eyed each person's condition. "Let's get acquainted."

One by one, each person introduced themselves.

"Hi, Walter, my name is Janene."

"Thank you for coming here, Walter. My name is Ron."

"I'm Karen."

"I'm so glad to see you, Walter. My name is Jackie."

"My name is Laura—brrr!"

"I'm Travis."

"My name is Jesse."

Walter was concerned. He knew that the party had been stranded in the unforgiving winds for a lengthy period. "Is everyone okay?" he asked.

Immediately the Scout leader spoke up. "This is all my fault," said Jackie. "We decided to take a different trail than what we originally planned—and then I lost my compass."

Walter noticed that Janene was holding the black book and saw that it had an imprint of a cross on its cover. Without thought, he pointed at the Good Book and said, "*This* is the only compass we'll be needing." His words did not fall upon deaf ears as the seven scouts looked at one another in agreement. All at once, a surge of energy was felt by all. One that gave an inner command, saying, *"Well c'mon, everyone. Let's get going!"*

In a reassuring voice, Walter said, "We are within an hour of a warm meal, fireplace and a place to stay the night."

That comment increased their will to survive. Everyone look at one another with encouragement. Walter was determined to guide them to safety, but not before restoring their body heat. The fire was his first concern. It needed to be rekindled as a necessity to rejuvenate numb faces, hands and feet. From there, he would make sure that all continued their trek wearing warm clothing. Once revived, he would take the stranded party and guide them to the *Never Never Land of Freeman County.*

"Let's get that fire built up," he said in a motivated tone.

The Eagle Scout had attended many survival courses and partook in his share of rescues. His expert eye already studied the bodies outlined in frost, and knew that their near-frozen jackets, socks, gloves, hats and scarfs had to be thawed out.

Walter walked to the nearby trees and, using his pocket knife, cut off tiny limbs. He masterfully built a dancing flame that enticed the Scouts to huddle around it. The larger twigs served as poles needed to suspend gloves and hats over the wavering heat.

Soon the campfire rose tall enough for cold faces, hands and feet to regain circulation. Woolen socks, neck scarfs and ski hats were also getting toasty. Walter wasn't finished, though. He reached into his father's old survival bag, and in moments a tin cup full of snow became hot chicken broth.

The fear of succumbing to a frozen death disappeared. There was now a tingling sensation throughout each and every body as the hot chicken broth was shared. Soon, each felt the same enthusiasm they had when they first embarked on this winter hike.

In time, without words being said, the seven hikers donned their socks and were soon dressed in warm gear. Seeing this, Walter acted fast. He knew that in actuality their bodies had taken quite a toll being stranded in the snowfield. He had achieved what was needed to get them moving, but also knew that they were too weak to travel any great length carrying a load. "It's best that we leave the backpacks here," he said. "All that's important is that we reach our destination. We can always come back later to get them."

The hikers had absolute trust in their hero and left their packs where they were resting. Quickly, Walter established the necessary movement needed to prevent their bodies from relapsing. Motioning his right arm, he gave the order. "Follow me." Without hesitation, the single-file line started to walk out of the clearing.

Walter had been properly trained by the great master himself: his father. Every step he took was based on the personal experiences his dad had passed onto him at campfires. Reflecting back, the hikes they went on and the bonding that took place amounted to saving seven lives that day. He looked quietly up to the sky and clenched a fist, whispering, "Thanks, Dad."

Troop 142 was re-energized thanks to Walter Rodman. Not only did he revive the Scouts, he renewed their spirits and gave them the will to move on.

There was more.

Unbeknownst to them, they would follow their Heavenly-sent Pied Piper to a legendary place they heard stories about...

The return trip seemed more beautiful to Walter because it was more gratifying. He knew that this scenic path was selected for him to perform as a servant. He was now returning with the utmost prized bounty: precious human life.

Ice formations, pristine meadows and curious wildlife were all waiting ahead. They were gifts from our Lord that would give

Walter a fuller sense of appreciation, knowing that this time he could share it with others.

The man smiled as his guests threw bread crumbs and birdseed toward hungry deer and fowl. They in turn were enjoying nourishing granola bars that maintained their strength. On occasion, a finger would point with the words, "Wow, look at that!" being spoken.

The hike didn't seem to take long at all with the final stretch being enhanced by signs that gave reassurance. It was the tantalizing aroma of baked bread that began to twitch noses as the famous bunkhouse came into view. Its fireplace would now guide them to salvation with its alder wood signature.

The charmed wooden fortress in the snow resembled a Thomas Kinkade painting that transported their souls back through time. Fond bedtime stories from Janene's childhood began to dance in her head, prompting her to smile. She now felt like Dorthy Gale discovering Oz, with her favorite dreams coming to life. It was obvious to her and the others where they were. Using her soft, inquisitive voice, she turned to Walter and asked, "Is this the Graves' house?"

Nightfall arrived at Freeman Valley, with record snowfalls continuing.

These life-threatening conditions were of no consequence, however. The spirit of the old bunkhouse on Coalman's Hill was alive as Troop 142 became the latest to find refuge there. In fact, this evening would go on to be the greatest campfire their lives would ever experience.

This episode began with Elizabeth opening the front door and inviting their guests inside. From there, quick introductions were made as Clara joined in. Walter ushered them to the change room that miners had once used a century ago. Updated plumbing allowed hot showers to be taken while their clothing cycled through the laundry. Their joyous mood became a makeshift circus, with everyone wearing unorthodox clown costumes.

Pajamas, robes, and sweat outfits were issued by household members to clothe their guests. The mismatched attire became a novelty that had everyone in stitches. Laughter erupted even louder when someone spotted their own image in a mirror.

Clara and Elizabeth were fully aware that their new friends were famished. They knew that the bread they baked that day would go perfect with stew. In no time at all, everyone was seated around the fireplace with full dinner trays on their laps.

The first round of storytelling was conveyed through silence. It came through the walls of the majestic structure, with its brass fittings and wooden floors setting the tempo. Earlier, Elizabeth herself gave the grand tour as curious looks absorbed the rich history. Each could sense the many hearts and souls that had graced the home with their presence, creating a century of stories that spread to dinner tables and bedrooms near and far.

Pictures of the Graves family surrounded them. Often, it was Elizabeth and her folklore papa staring back. "Papa will be back tomorrow, and then you can meet him," she said.

Dinner was finally finished, with a round of applause given to the chefs. Clara made a production out of it by taking Elizabeth by the hand with both giving a curtsey as if they were on stage.

The evening was just getting started. Coffee and cider were provided. "Later we'll have blackberry cobbler à la Mode," said Clara. This caused hands to rub tummies and tongues to outline lips.

Walter addressed an important issue that was being overlooked. "Hey, shouldn't we call your families and let them know you're okay?"

How right he was. It was a gamble for the seven Scouts to hike in the freezing temperatures—and now it was after dark. Walter held his fully charged cell phone up in the air and asked, "Any takers?"

Jackie grabbed the phone and started to dial. The phone was passed around the room, with comments like: "Mom, you're not going to believe this..." and, "Dad! Guess where we are?"

It was tied up for over an hour as the good news spread. Finally, the evening continued with every household rest assured that their loved ones were in the best hands imaginable.

The evening would now shift into high gear.

Walter brought out an antique popcorn popper. It was an iron mesh bowl that opened and closed tight at one end. It was secured shut with popcorn seeds inside and attached to a long pole. Walter noticed how fascinated Travis was by it and handed the utensil to him, asking, "Can you pop some corn for us?"

"Sure!" he eagerly replied. Travis immediately placed the seeds over the open flame and shook it slightly back and forth. In moments a popping sound filled the room as the meshed bowl filled with popcorn. At random, interesting stories circulated the room, with questions, ideas and occasional laughter following.

Soon Walter had another idea. "Let's get out that compass you were reading out of earlier today."

Clara and Elizabeth didn't understand what Walter meant by that comment, but Troop 142 certainly did. Jackie left the room and returned with the black book full of scriptures.

"Let's take turns reading out of it," suggested Karen.

"That sounds good to me," said Ron. "After all, it's never failed us yet!"

The very instrument credited for guiding the group to safety was now carrying them through the remainder of the evening. Like the classic song *Let it Snow,* everyone wished that their stay on Coalman's Hill would never end.

Let it snow, let it snow, let it snow...

Chapter XIV

CLAYTON GRAVES' SECOND VISIT with Dr. Schoenberg was definitely of a more serious nature. The legendary mountain man appeared weaker and checked into the hospital a few pounds lighter. That, along with the test results from his last visit, prompted the good doctor to explore even further.

Clayton knew that this was serious. He was already on prescription medicine, and more was being prescribed. His new friend was all business while conducting the tests. Once the results came back, Dr. Schoenberg wanted to have a personal one-on-one meeting with Clayton as soon as possible.

Together, they guesstimated when and where that would take place. They agreed to meet at Clayton's church on Coalman's Hill in two days, at ten in the morning.

"I can arrange to have a service there, and we can sit together," Clayton suggested.

"I would be honored!" replied the doctor.

The practitioner-turned-friend gave a professional handshake, followed by a hug that shared life.

The exchange with Jason was completed with Clayton leaving the city noise behind him. It was now time to enjoy the peaceful trip back through the enchanted winter-land and digest the recent events. Bundled up tight and sitting tall with his friend Desmond, they would follow Stardust back home. Hours passed with occasional snowfall, humorous stories and lapses of silence filled with prayer. Soon the familiar iron gates where friends and family resided came into view.

Nothing had to be said. Desmond knew where they were and showed the utmost respect. The deacon guided Stardust into the snow-covered lot and pulled back on the reins. The smooth gliding sleigh came to a halt, and Clayton tipped his hat to Desmond. "I found some chestnuts and pine cones this morning," he said. "They always add a nice touch to this neighborhood."

Desmond leaned back, gazing at the sky. He envisioned the beauty Clayton had just described and commented, "Tell everyone that I say hello."

The big man had already gotten out of the sleigh with his gifts. Walking toward the sacred monuments, he responded, "I surely will."

Silent flakes danced gracefully around the peaceful neighborhood as Clayton paid his respects. After a brief lapse of time, he returned with a somber look on his face.

"How is everyone?" asked Desmond.

His friend's humor tickled a funny bone that lifted his spirits. Looking up with his renowned smile, he said laughingly, "They're all just fine and send their regards."

Once aboard, Stardust surged forward to pull the sleigh toward Coalman's Hill. The sun was starting to set, turning mounds of white snow into gray shadows. All was fine, however, with nothing to fear. The power of prayer amongst the silence of falling snowflakes was all that was needed to get Clayton home.

In time, the smell of an alder wood fire reached out to them. It was the same scent that had spread methodically throughout the hills and forest for over one hundred years. The very one that offered refuge for anyone it touched, serving as an invitation to get out of the cold and be with loved ones.

Soon they were nearing the top of Coalman's Hill, and the structure from last century came into view. It resembled the Northern Star, casting its lights far and wide for all to see. Tonight a tradition would continue as an elated Clayton Graves would meet Troop Number 142.

Stardust had reached its destination, where a bowl of hay, apples and carrots served as dinner. That along with water, a sturdy stable, and the company of Cider made its work well worth the effort.

Inside was a typical evening at home, with new faces destined to become old friends. The legendary mountain man was anxious to see who the Lord sent to him that night—but first, he needed to change his clothing.

He entered the homestead and saw his lovely granddaughter conversing with their guests. All were in the living room, facing a roaring fire.

Only Walter spotted Clayton and Desmond, and gave a slight nod—one so inconspicuous that it didn't draw any attention to them. Desmond and Clayton nodded back in appreciation. They were wearing moist clothing that needed to be changed. That, along with a bar of soap and hot water, was first on their agenda. They quietly walked away to attend their business.

Desmond knew the routine and carried his duffel bag to the sleeping loft upstairs.

Walter left the group without saying anything. It appeared that it was for something menial, and that he would return shortly. Nothing needed to be said. Clayton went toward his bedroom with Walter a few steps behind. Just as he entered, Walter spoke up in a gentle tone. "Clayton."

Clayton was startled and turned to see his friend with a concerned look. Walter's soft voice and expressionless face telegraphed that there was something wrong. "What is it?" asked Clayton with compassion.

"Can we talk on the porch for a minute?" asked Walter.

Clayton paused for a moment, realizing that something of great importance was bothering his friend. "Sure," came his reply. "I'll meet you there in a moment," he said, patting Walter's shoulder.

Walter left quietly and found his way to the front porch without drawing any attention. Within minutes, Clayton arrived undetected in clean clothes and closed the door behind him. He stood inches from Walter and looked at him with his sincere brown eyes. "What's wrong?" he asked.

Walter looked directly at his friend and took a dry swallow. He obviously felt very uncomfortable as he began to spit out what he needed to say. "Look, I know that you trusted me to watch over things, but I couldn't help it."

Clayton was confused. To his knowledge, Walter had done nothing wrong. In fact, his friend *always* seemed to do everything right. "What on Earth are you talking about?" he asked in a loud whisper.

"Those people I took in while you were gone," he answered. In defense, he continued, "Look, they were lost attempting a winter hike and were about to get hypothermia when I found them. I had no choice but to..."

At that moment Clayton spoke in a slightly higher tone. With bulging eyes, he said, "That's what you were supposed to do! Don't you get it?" he asked. "Our Lord sent you there to save them! You were supposed to bring them here. God brought all of us here to be saved. This is *His* house, and we're to share it with everyone— just as you did!"

Emotions set in as Clayton wrapped his arms around Walter and hugged him. "I'm so proud of you, Walter. You were called upon to do the right thing, and you did just that!" Patting Walter on the back he repeated himself once again. "This is God's house, He led us all here."

A brief moment passed as Walter patted Clayton's back in return. It was a special moment that bonded the two men deeper. A testimony that adhered to their quest to further execute God's will. After a while, Clayton broke the silence with enthusiasm. Extending his arms straight out while still holding onto his friend, he exclaimed with bulging eyes, "Let's get in there, and you can introduce me to our new family members!"

Walter looked at the good man and said, "You're gonna like them!"

Once inside, the room stood still. All heads were turned to see The Mountain Man Of Coalman's Hill. The living legend who they'd heard many stories about—the man whose mere presence captivated any room.

Elizabeth was too proud to keep quiet and said, "That's my papa!" as she ran up to hug him.

Introductions were immediately made, followed by handshakes that became hugs. Soon many stories floated around, and laughter sweetened the pot. Janene, Ron, Karen, Jackie, Travis,

Jessie and Laura all expressed gratitude to Clayton for having his home open to them.

"My home?" questioned Clayton with a puzzled look on his face. "Before we moved in here, my family was in need just like yours," he explained. "This is God's house, and He's the one we need to thank!"

"He's right," said Walter with conviction.

"This *is* God's house."

Silence filled the room, with all realizing how right he was. Without thought, everyone gathered around the fireplace and held hands forming a circle. Elizabeth opened with her message of thanks to our Creator. To her left and around the room, one by one, each gave their thanks.

Once finished, there was more silence until Clara spoke up. "Hey, we need some more popcorn!"

"And some cocoa and hot cider," added Elizabeth.

As it was a century ago, the living room was in full swing as new faces became friends—and then family.

Chapter XV

THE FOLLOWING MORNING showed more signs that were uncharacteristic of Clayton Graves. The tired man who tried his best to hide his illness couldn't wake up until Elizabeth shook his arm repetitively crying out, "Papa, Papa, it's time to get up!"

His weathered face, darkened eyes and rumbling cough caused her to panic. She might have only been seven-years-old, but his recent trips to the big city, abrupt change in appearance and those whispering about him gave her reason to fear. "Are you okay, Papa?"

Papa mustered up all the strength he had, and after a few more throat-clearing hacks, turned on his side and faced her.

"I'm just fine, darling," he said with a smile.

"Papa," she exclaimed, "Clara and I made breakfast for everyone. After that, we want you to take us down the hill. We told our new friends about it and they want to go down the hill with you!"

Clayton had no concern about his condition at that moment. He saw the joy in the child's eyes and could never refuse her.

Anxiously she looked back at her papa and jumped up and down pleading, "Can we, Papa? Can we?"

"We sure can," he said with his soft heart. "Let me get up and sample what you and Clara cooked this morning, then we'll hit the slopes."

Elizabeth surged at the man she loved and wrapped her arms around his head, yelling, "Yeah!"

Clayton was in the kitchen enjoying Swedish pancakes with oatmeal. That along with butter, maple syrup, raisins, milk and brown sugar covered all the bases. Equally important, a robust cup of coffee sat in front of him—all served by his favorite server, Elizabeth.

Clayton's mouth opened wide as he stared in disbelief at the feast that was before him. "My, my," he said as he looked at his proud granddaughter. "Did you and Clara really cook this?"

A proud Elizabeth stood straight and nodded her smiling face up and down many times.

Walter entered the kitchen and said, "You and Clara did another fantastic job in the kitchen! Let me clean everything up."

Elizabeth knew a good deal when she heard one. "Okay," she said in an agreeable tone. "I'll go outside and play in the snow until Papa gets out there."

Clayton loved her spirit and said, "As soon as I finish this awesome, incredible, delicious meal, I'll hurry up and get changed."

An excited little girl said, "Okay, Papa; I'll tell everyone!" The energetic child dashed out of the kitchen.

"Well, someone is certainly happy," commented Walter. With coffee cup in hand, he sat across from Clayton and asked, "How do you feel this morning?"

Clayton had just taken a swallow and said, "I'm a little weak, but should make it through the day."

"Are you really going to sled down the hill today?" asked his concerned friend. "It's deeper out there, because it snowed again last night. Besides, you are fighting something."

Clayton took a sip of coffee and placed the cup on a coaster. Looking at Walter, he gave his answer. "I need to," he said. "It keeps the young man inside me alive."

Walter fully understood that what Clayton had just said was the truth. He excused himself from the table and got up to leave, saying, "See ya outside." He knew that Clayton had a lot on his mind and needed time to himself.

❧❧❧

The toboggan was packed solid as Troop Number 142 did everything possible to scrunch in like a can of sardines.

Elizabeth was now called to duty.

It was her watch, and all knew that her authorization was needed for clearance. Standing tall, she peered over the curved shield and scanned their surroundings from side to side, both near and far. Despite the display of light snowflakes falling everywhere, she saw well enough to guarantee that their path had no obstructions. It was simply layered with another sprinkle of precious crystals.

Without hesitation, she sat down and snuggled into the tight quarters. "We can go!" came the command.

Walter and his wife didn't want to miss out on the fun. They volunteered to give the push needed to send them downhill. It wouldn't take much, however, since the massive toboggan was resting at the crest of the hill. Next, Walter would lay down on a sled with Clara giving a little push, laying on top of him—and hanging on for dear life!

Walter pushed the toboggan and quickly laid down on his sled. Clara then gave him a push and barely got on as the sled took off.

The ride was underway, with none other than Clayton Graves himself commanding the ship. The old man still had it and masterfully took control as the toboggan gained speed. Elizabeth was wedged in the front, much tighter than ever before with both hands in the air as Troop Number 142 *screamed* with excitement!

Not far behind was the team of Walter and Clara Rodman, zig-zagging like Olympians. It was another breathtaking, exhilarating, fun-filled ride, where everyone felt like they were a rocket blasting down a mountainside!

Once at the bottom, expressions like:

"Wow!"

"Oh my word!"

"Amazing!"

"Incredible!"

"I can't believe it!" echoed all about.

Tradition continued with the friendly jest of snow dust thrown above others—but not *at* them. It took the scouts a millisecond to see and understand *why* as they joined in. Snow dust was falling everywhere as larger flakes continued to fall. It was young and old united and playing like children. In time, the thrill that came from having the ride of a lifetime began to die down as reality faced them.

It was the moment of truth: getting everything and everyone up the hill and back home- including Clayton.

Ron, Janene, Jessie, Travis, Jackie, Karen and Laura were already two steps ahead. When they first entered the fabled bunkhouse, they saw the many pictures that choreographed the man's life. Upon seeing him a rude awakening set in. It was obvious that his hard work ethic and many years of self-sacrificing had taken a toll. Naturally, they were aware how lucky they were to meet him, especially with the realization that he wouldn't be around much longer.

Methodically they made a human chain that secured Clayton as they took one step at a time to climb the hill. A rope was secured waist-high around the group that pulled the toboggan, with the smaller sled fastened behind. Inside was Elizabeth, being Queen of the Nile.

They made it up the hill where a rekindled fire awaited. Hot cider and stories would fill the rest of the day as a hearty stew simmered on the back burner.

The snowfall escalated into a blizzard keeping the local schools and most businesses closed. This enclosure only enhanced the harmony inside the bunkhouse on Coalman's Hill. Everyone was warm and happy inside with the technology of a modern-day cell phone at their fingertips.

Important calls were made to families to confirm that all were okay. In fact, they announced that the group had voted unanimously to stay another night at the Graves' house. It was understood that they would attend a church service the following morning at ten and then call their families to discuss getting home.

Clayton couldn't wait until church services started. He would be sitting next to his new friend, Johann and later would confer with Dr. Schoenberg.

I wonder what he's got for me tomorrow? thought Clayton as he went to bed.

Chapter XVI

ELIZABETH SHOOK HER GRANDFATHER'S arm while profusely saying, "Wake up, Papa, wake up!" It was hours after sunrise, the normal time Clayton Graves usually rose from bed. Immediately, involuntary coughing and wheezing took control of his body as he shook with sweat. This fit lasted for a while and got worse before it resided. Elizabeth was scared. "Are you gonna die, Papa?"

The aging grandfather dug deep within himself and found the strength and courage needed to answer her properly. Rolling onto his side, he said, "Who, me? I'm just getting a little old; that's all."

The sparkle in his eye was enough to pacify the child. "Clara and I made another breakfast," she said. "You need to hurry up so that we can make it to church on time."

Clayton was quick and said, "Now when is a commander ever late?"

His strength was present, which was what Elizabeth needed to see. Hugging him, she said, "I love you, Papa."

It was almost ten o'clock with Clayton Graves sitting next to one Johann Michael Schoenberg. One might ask: how could a city boy arrive in all that snow?

The answer: Desmond Miller was sitting next to him, and Stardust was tethered outside.

Pastor Moore approached the pulpit and gazed at his friend, Clayton. Next he nodded thanks at Desmond for bringing the good doctor and then scanned at a few others who were scattered about. The service was another homemade recipe that the church provided for the snow-bound community. It spread the word of God while leaving its doors open for anyone who needed comfort or shelter. This was the standard that the Graves' house always

88

followed. The sermon was fitting for the occasion and seemingly tailor-made for Clayton Graves in particular.

The pastor talked about our Lord giving us the gift of life so that we could serve Him like an obedient soldier. Those words hit Clayton like a ton of bricks as the holy man looked directly at him. He went on to talk about life and spent a good half-hour going into detail on *why* it's so important to put others first—a trademark of Clayton Charles Graves.

When the services finally came to an end, an idea instantaneously crossed Clayton's mind. It had just occurred to him that Desmond had an empty sleigh, and his newly formed friends needed to find a way down the mountainside.

It all made sense as he looked above with his hands spread out. *Thank you, my Lord* was the message sent in return.

Clayton bounced the idea off Desmond with the deacon saying, "I thought God was sending me here to do a little extra today."

Jackie was then presented the idea and said, "That will work out perfectly!" The hikers had even brought their belongings with them to church as a safeguard. Jackie told the others, and calls were made. Everyone knew of the road that led up to Coalman's Hill. It was just a matter of riding down the fluffy powder until the family vehicle with chains was spotted.

While the trip was being carefully coordinated, Johann became Dr. Schoenberg and looked at Clayton with a serious expression that showed great sadness.

It was time for their heart-to-heart, and Clayton was prepared for the worst. He excused himself and led the doctor to a private room that had a table with a few chairs. "I suppose this is as good of a place as any," said Clayton as he closed the door behind them.

Each took a seat facing one another. Clayton sat back as Dr. Schoenberg rested his elbows on the table. With hands clasping the sides of his face, he looked down with eyes closed. It was an uncomfortable situation, as if Johann had been brought in by a detective to be interrogated.

More time passed until Clayton broke the silence. "Which one of us is the patient, anyway?"

Emotionally, Dr. Johann Michael Schoenberg had hit bottom—but Clayton's sense of humor was the best medicine. He couldn't help but laugh as he raised his head to look at the dying man.

The sickly eyes and frail body showed courage as he patiently waited for the news.

"Clayton," said the doctor as sincere blue eyes peered through his glasses. "This is the hardest part of my profession..."

"Well then, just say it," said the decorated military man. "We'll still be friends anyway."

Leaning back in the chair, he folded his arms and went into 'automatic'. "You see, Clayton; it's like a car..."

If there ever was an insult that reached out to Clayton Graves in recent years, it was that.

The almighty 'car analogy' had been the oldest form of weak explanation since its invention. *It's always been a guy's way out* his father would tell him. True, he knew that Johann loved him and didn't know *how* to deliver such bad news to a special friend. Still, he was greatly disappointed and had to deduct points.

Despite Clayton's life being the one at stake, he understood his friend's pain and accepted Johann's lack of imagination. Once again, it was time to hear about how something—anything—was like a car...

Clayton folded his arms and relaxed until the memorized filibuster had finally come to an end. By that time, it was *professionally* delivered that he was diagnosed with late stages of cancer.

What Clayton and others feared had become a reality. Without batting an eye, he asked the next obvious question.

"How much time do I have, Doc?"

Dr, Schoenberg showed signs of getting more and more uncomfortable as he fidgeted and stared down. After a long pause, he said in a quivering voice, "Not very long; we've done all that we could..."

Clayton arrived expecting the worst and got just that. He stood up and rested his right hand on Johann's shoulder saying, "It's not your fault. You did all that you could." The terminal patient left the room without anything else needing to be said. Once outside, he was greeted by Walter and Pastor Moore. He broke the news to them and asked if he could be alone at home for a day or two to sort things out. "I would appreciate it if you and your wife wouldn't mind staying here with Elizabeth until I give you a call," he requested.

"Not at all," said Walter.

"Just tell her that I have some chores to do, and that I'll be with her real soon," he added.

"We'll do just that," replied Walter.

At that moment, Jackie and his troop approached the three men with an update. "We're all set," he said in a tone of relief. "My brother understands where we are and is going to meet us about two miles down the road. He has an old International fitted with chains that will get the job done. Desmond says that his sleigh has enough room for all of us and our gear—and that he has to go that way anyway." Jackie was almost delirious over the good news. "Can you believe that?" he practically yelled out. "How can anybody get so lucky?"

Clayton pushed his problem aside and asked a question. "Have you been praying since you were stranded out in the snow?"

Jackie was quick to respond. "Praying?" he asked in a felicitous tone. "Why, we haven't stopped praying since..." At that precise moment something dawned on him that explained *everything*. He looked at Janene, then Laura, Jessie, Travis, Karen and Ron as the message sank in. Slowly he looked at Clayton, and in a humble tone said, "We were praying the whole time."

There was a brief moment of silence as heads nodded with the understanding of *how* they really got there. Walter broke the silence by handing Jackie something he had left behind in the pew. It was a leather-bound black book of Godly pages, the same one that he and his fellow scout members were reading when he first found them. "You left your compass behind," he said with a little laugh.

"Thanks," said Jackie as he took possession of the Good Book. "You can never get lost with one of these!"

Finally, farewells and gratitude were exchanged. Everyone finished up by telling Clayton how much they loved him. Desmond then led the scouting troop to his sleigh.

The ride down the mountainside was joyous to say the least. Stardust easily pulled the sleigh as the beauty of God's frozen creation was topped with more radiant snow.

Eventually a classic International dressed for the conditions was seen off to the side with its high beams flickering. Just as planned, Jackie's brother, Mathew was there to take the party back home. There was a stipulation that needed to be addressed, however. When they came within one hundred yards of the vehicle, it was agreed that Stardust would come to a halt. Troop Number 142 got out of the sleigh and walked the final stretch with dignity.

Cider pulled Clayton's sleigh up the mountain road they had traveled down earlier. Alone and with lots on his mind, he decided to take a brief hike to a place that few knew of—a special place that was maybe a quarter of a mile or so from the bunkhouse. When the massive wooden structure came into view, he had Cider take a sharp left. What one initially saw was a thick cluster of trees that together made a rock formation look like a gigantic Christmas tree. Even at close range, it appeared that this community could only harbor insects and select wildlife. It wasn't until one actually crawled under the right set of overlapping branches that its secret was unveiled.

Inside was a naturally hidden path that resembled a spiral staircase made of rock. Tall, bushy trees and overhanging ledges kept this tight formation relatively shielded from the elements. It would even allow a dying man to climb it during the winter months.

All Clayton needed to do was find the right branches, look around to see if anyone was watching, then scurry underneath them like a rodent. The mountain man knew exactly where he was; after all, throughout his life he knew to come here when he needed absolute solitude.

He looked in all directions with caution. Abruptly he dropped to his knees and began to burrow under the snow-covered branches. A few limbs swayed, dropping armfuls of snow on Clayton's back. That wasn't enough to stop Commander Graves as he used a military maneuver to elbow his way across. He was now inside the protective foliage, where standing room was allowed. He got up anxiously as the snow fell off of his back. To his delight, the almost completely dark, hidden refuge remained unchanged.

In front of him, he could barely see a series of natural overlapping slabs of granite and flat rocks that allowed one to walk on. The jagged wall it outlined, along with the thick vegetation that covered its exterior, would serve as a convenient hand railing. Clayton cautiously grabbed onto protruding rocks that were at eye level with one hand and branches with the other. Pulling on limbs and grabbing the jagged wall, he slowly climbed the slippery rocks with secured steps.

The primitive stairwell was cumbersome, but it did serve its purpose. The higher he climbed, the tighter the radius became. On occasion his age and condition would catch up to him, causing the sixty-two-year-old cancer patient to catch his breath. The dull lighting that initially made seeing almost impossible gradually became brighter as he ascended toward the top. It was as if he were at the bottom of the ocean and reaching the surface.

Eventually Clayton could see a burst of light, accompanied by an intense Arctic chill. He was nearing the top, with just a few more treacherous steps to conquer.

Finally his methodical footing reached the top, where untouched snow rested on top of and in between boulders. He persevered through the deep snow and narrow passageway to find what he was looking for.

There before him, it came into view.

On a ledge surrounded by alpine trees was an evenly snow-covered wooden bench that his dad and grandfather had built over fifty years ago. He approached it knowing that his nylon snow suit could accept the bench just the way it was. Without a worry, the tired man sat down at the highest peak of Coalman's Hill and gazed at the abandoned coalmine below.

This was a secret place that his dad and grandfather had introduced to him. It was understood that this special place was only to be known by them, God, and especially the natural citizens originally put there: wildlife and the Native Americans.

Clayton felt honored that he was allowed to be a part of this. Often, he felt that he was an eagle reporting to our Lord when he ventured there. The crisp chill in the air and undisturbed setting before him brought a feeling of tranquility that allowed him to reflect on his life.

Without warning, a voice addressed Clayton, startling him beyond belief.

"How much time did they give you?"

Chapter XVII

CLAYTON'S HEART SKIPPED A BEAT with him almost jumping out of his seat. It was the initial shock of being one with nature and the belief that only God was present. With regard to the distinct voice that pierced the quiet setting, he knew who it belonged to and responded.

"You gotta stop sneaking up on me like that, Pete. I almost died from a heart attack—again!"

Turning around, he saw the strong, noble face with distinct cheekbones and dynamic black hair wearing a buckskin jacket. It was his fellow mountain man, Pete Rainwater with his ancestral traits ever present. A being whose culture was originally gifted this land.

Clayton was stunned that word had traveled so fast and asked, "How did you know about my condition?"

Pete's face remained expressionless as he looked over the bluff. "I'm Native American," he said. "I have sensed for some time that you were ill."

Clayton answered the question in a deadpan voice. "My doctor told me that my time is near."

"Did he use the one about being like a car?" Pete asked in a sarcastic tone.

"He most certainly did," replied Clayton.

Pete's demeanor turned into one of theatrics. Spreading his arms out as if to encompass the entire world, he asked in a loud voice, "Why do they *still* use that one?" He stepped forward in front of Clayton and continued. "Does everything always have to be like a car?" he asked with hand movements. Looking up to the sky he raised his arms. "Why can't they come up with something original?"

Pete turned to address his friend further. "Do you know what I get all the time?" he asked with a confused expression. Answering his own question he said, "When some of them meet me for the first time, they want me to know that they know someone who's *Cherokee*." Spinning around with his arms extended he yelled, "Now what does *that* have to do with anything?"

Pete had more.

The local resident pulled up a sleeve on his jacket and exposed brown skin with its mild red hue. Next, he forcibly took off one of Clayton's gloves and held his bare arm next to his rich black hand. Talking between the lines, Pete asked another sensitive question.

"Did he do the one about—you know, some of his best friends being...?"

Clayton picked up on that one fast and said, "No, but he might have been going there if I didn't leave when I did." He put his glove back on.

Each shook their head in disappointment as a silent lapse took place. Finally, Pete changed topics. "My ancestors tipped me off about your condition, but say that you still have some time here with us," he said. "That's because there is a thing or two you need to finish before you are allowed in..."

Those words touched Clayton and registered deep. He thought for a while about what loose ends he needed to tie up while he still had precious life. At once, it hit him like a ton of bricks. Down below was the stump where he and his friends always gathered to see who would be *The King of Coalman's Hill.*" Slowly a smile came across his face, knowing that he had at least one more attempt to regain his crown.

Looking over, he saw that Pete had vanished. The spiritual mountain man had left undetected, just as he arrived.

Clayton looked back at the stump below and felt a surge of energy.

The walk down the rocky steps was much easier for Clayton, and soon he was riding home. Cider was eventually back in its stable being fed, while Clayton was inside inspecting the Graves Express. It had been serviced since its last record attempt and was indeed ship-shape, ready to go. There was vigor in every step the old man took, as if he was his good ol' self. He even warmed up a bowl of stew and added saltine crackers. He was feeling stronger, and appeared to be the man he used to be.

Looking out his living room window, he could see that the soft gray clouds still held a haze of daylight. This signaled that there was ample time to make a record attempt. He donned his battle gear and, with stopwatch in hand, carried the Graves Express to the forum.

He stood next to the stump and briefly acknowledged those he felt were present. Looking down the course, he saw what he was hoping for. The recent ride in the overloaded toboggan had left a flattened path that was glazed over with ice. Fresh snow seemed to provide a nurturing layer of powder, allowing the right depth for steering. If there was ever a perfect condition to attempt a record run on Coalman's Hill, it was *now*.

Quietly, he gave his undivided attention to his mental checklist one last time:

>Runners straight and waxed.
>Steering mechanism working perfectly.
>Watch wound and ready to be activated.
>Bootlaces tied.
>Neck scarf tied properly.
>Gloves on proper hands.
>Woolen beanie on tight.

Everything checked out. Next, the famed Flexible Flyer was meticulously positioned evenly with the stump. Finally, our hero climbed on board face down with his gloved index finger ready to click on the second hand. It was just a matter of time as he waited for the spiritual clearance.

It came.

The light snow flurry took a moment of rest, as a mighty gust of wind came from nowhere. It blew mysteriously down the track as if to clean it. Clayton secured the timepiece in his left hand and used his right to lunge the sled forward and break the crest of the hill. In doing so, he pressed down on the second hand and felt it click, starting the timer.

This perfect day came with a bonus. He felt the unmistakable force of many hands push down on his body and violently shove him forward; resembling a circus performer being shot out of a cannon.

Already he was flying through the first turn instinctively dragging his opposite foot to help guide the runaway sled. With both feet back in their natural positions, he straightened out only to hit the second turn with full force. Clayton had to scrape the opposite side at least once with his other foot to avoid flying up and over the icy embankment.

He made it, as the steel runners covered the frozen ground faster and faster! Keeping a cool head, he straightened out the Graves Express and realized there were no dark shadows that forewarned of the usual bumps that had to be avoided. The path laid out from the toboggan ride smoothed out the trail like fresh blacktop. It was all a red carpet!

Clayton approached the metal stretch that could easily accelerate him into orbit. He went over it like a shot, straight and true, and stopped the second hand as he blurred through the open gates. Protecting the heirloom and its precious reading, he covered it with both hands. He knew that the rolling beds of powder would stop the sled—and even catch him if needed. The errant sled was now drifting aimlessly as it went uphill, partially burying itself in a haystack of forgiving snow. The erratic ride threw Clayton off before impact, with the prized stopwatch protected.

He was now face-up and lying in the comforts of a fluffy snowbank. Clayton was okay as he breathed heavily. The rejuvenated man remained still and contemplated what had just happened. Next he remembered *why* he was there, and looked at his clasped gloves.

Fear crossed his mind as he hoped that his flight downhill hadn't caused any damage to the stopwatch. He stood up carefully and closed his eyes. With courage he opened his hands and looked down to see that it was intact and in a stopped position. Suspense mounted as he positioned the instrument where daylight would expose its face allowing him to read what it had recorded.

His time?

An astounding eighteen seconds—and a new record!

Clayton Charles Graves cleared his throat in disbelief. Carefully, he closed the antique timepiece and placed it into his coat pocket, knowing that it would *never* be used again.

He paused a bit longer to let his victory set in, then at once raised both arms and jumped in victory.

"I did it!" echoed the king's voice throughout the hill. Warm with sweat, he felt bulletproof. Next would be a tradition to adhere to. On top, at the very stump where they always gathered, court would be in session to crown the new king. Clayton's strength remained as he found the sled and towed it up the polished slope crying out, "I did it! I did it!"

Once on top, his composure leveled off. The procession was about to begin. It was time to greet his subjects and follow etiquette.

Using a thick British accent, he began by giving a formal bow to each of his subjects as he addressed them. He pivoted with hands at his sides as each member of their royal family was mentioned.

"Sir Rolland, it's so good to see you today, old man."

"Sir Earl, you're looking good today, ol' chap."

"Sir Charles, just lovely to see you today."

"Sir Carlton, glad you are here, old boy."

"Sir Daryl, nice to see that you brought your squire here with you."

"Squire Melven, pip-pip, ol' bean."

"Sir Horace, we must do tea time."

With the formalities out of the way, it was now time for the new record holder to be crowned 'King Of Coalman's Hill'.

Down on one knee with head bowed, he touched each shoulder where the royal ceremonial sword would have touched. The imaginary crown was now being placed on his head for all to see as he said, "Oh, that fits just lovely; just lovely, my dear..."

The new king was crowned as he stood up and gave more bows from side to side. Next he spun around, waving his imaginary gallant robe for the entire kingdom to see. The ceremony was complete prompting Clayton to leave with a swagger. "Ta-ta, my dears," he said while making his exit.

Once home, he rested the Graves Express next to the front door and took off his gloves, scarf, jacket and cap. From there he wasted no time entering his bedroom and pushed an awaiting thumbtack into the wall. There he hung the immortal timepiece, with its protective covering open. The historical moment would now be forever frozen in time.

Clayton stood back and gazed at the tarnished watch with pride. He took a step closer and marveled at the hands that would never move again...the ones that read 'eighteen seconds'.

At that moment he began to feel nauseous and started to sweat profusely. Feeling immense pain within his stomach, he covered it with both hands and ran to the bathroom. Once there, he knelt down in front of the toilet and coughed up blood.

Chapter XVIII

MORNING WAS A HAPPY OCCASION at the Freeland Community Church.

It seemed word had gotten around that if you could make it to the church at the foothills of Coalman's Hill, you'd have the time of your life! School was still closed due to the heavy snowfall—but church was *always* open.

More faces trickled in, with some belonging to newcomers. There were even those who were out of money and made the trek just to survive. Pastor Moore would greet such people, making them aware that they were *always* welcome.

Clara Rodman was definitely a huge draw. Recently she had volunteered to go far and wide to assist any and all youth programs affiliated with the church. She not only filled out the forms needed; she also included a biography about herself stating her background and interests. It resembled a brochure and especially covered her devotion to God and the love she had for children. Pastor Moore made copies of it and included it with his monthly flier.

Like a boomerang, her message of good will came back with an influx of youth from all walks of life seeking her.

Comments like, "I bet you're Clara Rodman!" "Are you Clara?" "Are you Mrs. Rodman?" and, "Clara, I came here to meet you!" were known to bombard her from all sides.

Walter loved it. For decades he felt that he had let his wife down by not fathering children. Now, she technically had ten times more than anyone they knew—and they *loved* it!

Pastor Moore was happy because the church was now serving its purpose by having more calling it *home.*

Elizabeth was the most proud. She had told all of her friends about Clara, and was now making more friends! There was also an inner peace within the child. She was made aware of her papa's absence, but it wasn't because of another hospital trip. It was because he just needed to be home for a while to rest and take care of some menial chores...

Clayton was grateful that he had the place to himself. His seesaw battle with cancer seemed to get better, and then nosedive. That morning he slept in late and again woke up sickly. He thanked God that Elizabeth wasn't there to see him.

He rested in bed for another hour until he felt strong enough to get up. From there he looked at the hands of his uncle's old stopwatch and saw that they were unchanged. The magnificent display boosted his strength, allowing him to change into warm clothes and stoke the living room fire that still glowed. His appetite was nonexistent that morning, but Clayton brewed some coffee out of habit—a pot he didn't even drink out of.

Looking outside, he watched yet another flurry fall from the sky. This set the tone for his thoughts to be channeled to the utmost highest level our lives could possibly conceive: Our Creator, why we're here and what He needs from us.

Throughout his entire life, Clayton Graves had the good fortune of having parents who had done a masterful job guiding him. It all stemmed from being compassionate toward others, with the good Lord's word guiding the way.

"Never stop praying," his mother always said. "God always hears you."

"Our Lord *will* hand you what you want at times," said his dad. "It's just a biscuit to keep you on the path he has meant for you. It's all a Heavenly path," he would explain.

True, he'd been granted the necessary tools needed to conquer the hill before being united with his friends once again. Still, there was something far more important that needed to be addressed. Something pressing that consumed his every waking moment: Elizabeth's welfare.

Clayton Charles Graves knew that his passing was inevitable. But still, he didn't want to leave the sole survivor of the Graves family behind at such a young age. Always the diplomat, it was time for him to go outside, get comfortable, and barter with the miracle maker Himself: God.

It took much of the day to reach the bench that his dad and grandfather built long ago. Health-wise, he was stripped of the excessive youth given the day before, reducing him to the ailing patient that he was.

In time he was sitting with the abandoned mine, his childhood, and all of creation before him. The stage was set with winter's silence and graceful flakes fluttering about.

Taking his time, Clayton gathered his thoughts and remained calm. He stared down and kept his eyes closed to piece together and rehearse what he needed to say—and in what order. The old man felt that he needed to put his best foot forward and back up his request with facts. He wanted a perfect delivery in order to be potent enough to sway things in his favor.

Poised and ready to go, he began to address the Supreme Judge. Clayton chose to start off his pitch with a cute, lovable smile that came with a twinkle in his eye, a likeable image that reminded one of Fred Sanford.

"My Lord, you've always been there for me..."

Clayton's words dissipated in the thin mountain air. He sat still and paused momentarily while selecting the choice words he would use next. "I realize that you already know why I'm here," he added.

Leaning forward, he clasped his hands together and rested them on his lap. He realized that a prepared speech wasn't needed. God already *knew* who he was—and loved him and *everyone* beyond words. Furthermore, our Creator always listened to his and everyone's prayers, regardless of how small they may appear.

He knew what was going on.

Clayton took off his mask and simply began to express himself. "Who am I trying to kid?" he commented as he burst out laughing. "But I'm still going to ask another favor out of ya!" he added shaking an index finger at the sky. Without warning, the old man leaned over due to involuntary coughing. When he felt stable, he cleared his throat and sat straight up. Without any thought, he began to talk like Clayton Graves.

"My entire life has been blessed because of you," he said in a groggy voice.

"I'll never forget the time at Thompson's Creek when it was swamped with families trying to catch *anything* to eat. You gave me a notion that I should go there that day, and to bring my pole." He bent over and resumed a coughing fit that made him feel lightheaded. Once recovered, he sat up again and continued to address the Lord.

"When I got there, I saw that no one was getting a bite.

"You were very aware that *I* knew how to fish that creek—and once I got my line in the water; I was catching those catfish left and right." Clayton started to shake his index finger toward the clouds as he projected his voice. "It's like your bible stories: Through your grace, I was able to feed many. We were a team!" he exclaimed, standing up with a raised fist. Sitting back down, he went further.

"I also want to point out that those very people were invited to the home you allowed my granddaughter and I to live in. We know that it's actually *your* home; and it's there to be shared with anyone in need." Clayton squinted his eyes as he assembled the thought he was trying to convey.

"That old bunkhouse was so full that I called some of my friends to come over—including Pastor Moore. I let them know what *you* did for everyone, and that we were going to have a big fish fry that night." Standing up again, he pointed his finger directly ahead and spoke.

"Everyone got to know one another that night, with the pastor leading us in prayer and blessing the meal. After dinner I brought our new friends to my barn and gave them bags to take as many army rations as they needed for their families. My shelves were emptied, but over time you did fill them up again."

It was now time for the best part of the story.

"Well, Lord you know what happened next. The following day was Sunday, and Pastor Moore invited our guests to his church service. Everyone was there on Sunday morning, with each and every one of them joining *your* church..."

Clayton had to catch his breath as more events surfaced. He went on to mention of the many times a Doubting Thomas saw the light and joined their congregation. The times souls with a dark past had nowhere else to go but to the church at the foothills of Coalman's Hill—and got baptized. He pointed out those who'd lost their will to live, until they found salvation.

"We've had lots of seniors who felt they were forgotten and gave up all hope, until we found them," he said.

Clayton shifted gears and focused on Elizabeth. "You are the only one who would actually understand what my granddaughter means to my life." Holding his hands together like an altar boy in prayer, he lowered his head. "And I will never question you as to why I have lost my family members one by one. I have also never lost sight of the many wonderful people that you have put in our lives, who are just like family."

Looking up, his tense face was shedding tears as he pleaded, "Please, Lord, please. I need to live longer; *much* longer. She is too young to continue life without any of her real family with her."

With a running nose and a trembling voice that resembled hiccups, he marched on. "Look, I know that I've asked a lot from you before, and that you were probably performing miracles for me. I never forgot the times my men and I were in battle, and I thought that we wouldn't make it out alive—but we did. I always honored the lives that you created and only meant to shoot *toward* our opposing soldiers—and not actually *at* them. I knew that you had us there for the right reasons, and that we had to give respect in return."

Clayton began to get frustrated as he put his hands on the sides of his head. There was more to be said. "I have never feared death before, because I have always lived for you. But this time it's different. Before, I was proud to put my life on the line and defend what you stood for. Now I want to live and take care of the child I know *you* put me here to watch over."

Clayton had one final statement to make. "If I could have my way, I'd outlive her so that she would always have her papa there for her."

Emotionally Clayton was expired after voicing his request to God. The good man finished with: "Thank you, Lord for hearing my prayer."

Silence continued as snowflakes swirled in the mild breeze. A familiar, unexpected sound from behind reminded Clayton that someone else also lived in those parts.

"Was that an eighteen-second run I saw you do yesterday?"

One would think that Clayton Charles Graves would come to expect his Native American friend to always be there when all seemed still. In a brief state of panic, he twitched as if being electrocuted. Once he calmed down, Clayton said, "Yer gonna kill me, Pete..." Having regained his composure, he answered the question. "That was an eighteen-second pass, all right."

Pete went crazy. "I thought so!" he exclaimed in a jubilant tone as he danced around. Standing next to Clayton, he asked, "What was the old record; twenty-three seconds or something like that?"

The old man turned and looked at him with an amazed expression. "You're right again," he said. "How do you know these things?" asked Clayton as he shook his head in wonderment.

"From up here," he said with an element of pride in his voice. "Man," he continued, "I *always* rooted for you!"

Pete went into specifics. Pacing around with head lowered, he raised his arms and started to explain:

"There were times when—geez, ya almost had it..." Pivoting around, he pointed at his friend and elaborated further. "I mean, you came close so many times—and then something would get ya."

Pete began to go back through the years and report what he saw.

"There was this one time when you just had to keep it straight, and the record would have been yours. You hit a bump and flew to the right, cartwheeling into a snowbank and messing up your sled. The next time out, you hit the same bump on the other side and did the same thing going the other way. But I knew you'd be back."

There was more.

"Once you were almost at the finish line and then a runner came off. Another time you were on pace until your right boot came off when you tried to turn. But you did it yesterday, brother, and I'm *so* proud of you! I knew that you were going to get your title back!" he said, swinging a fist like Joe Lewis.

"Yer the man!" he said in praise.

Clayton started to blush as he nodded in agreement. With his chest puffed out, he gazed at the slope he'd conquered the day before and beamed with pride.

Pete changed topics. "Your prayers travel on the same wavelength my meditation does. Whether it's God, the Great Spirit or our Lord; it's all been heard, and things are going on up there." The wise Native looked directly at him, saying, "My ancestors are all talking about you. Something major is going to happen soon— trust me." Pete had one more thing to say. "The gates are beginning to open..."

Clayton lowered his head with eyes closed as he digested his friend's words. They left him speechless as he turned to look at him.

Pete Rainwater was gone.

Chapter XIX

CLAYTON'S WEARY BODY struggled to make it home. Nightfall found him in front of the fireplace, reflecting back on the day's mission. He realized that the first sign of being granted an extended life would be to feel strength enter his deteriorating body.

He felt no such change. In fact, he was feeling weaker and had vomited more blood earlier. *I'll just give the Lord more time*, he concluded.

The phone rang. It was his friend Walter checking up on him. "Clayton, how are you feeling today?" he asked.

Clayton's faint voice painted a bad picture as he coughed during his response. "I'm determined to get better. How are things at church?"

"We miss you," said Walter. "Other than that, we're having a ball. You know what happens around here."

"How's Elizabeth?" asked the grandfather.

" *Well*," replied Walter in a high-pitched voice. "Your little girl gave us a scare this morning."

Alarmed, Clayton asked, "What happened? Is she all right?"

Walter took control. "She's just fine." he said. "Last night she fainted—but Clara was on top of things. Elizabeth didn't get hurt, and Clara placed her in bed with a damp cloth over her forehead. When she came to, she didn't even remember doing it."

"She must have been tired from all of the activities going on," said Clayton.

"That's what we thought," agreed Walter. "Don't worry, though. We're playing it safe and keeping a close eye on her. We also know that the patient will feel ten times better when she sees her papa."

"Good," said Clayton with a chuckle. "Because that's what I need to feel better!"

"Would you like more time alone, or should we come back home?" asked Walter.

"By all means, come home," replied Clayton. "It's getting too quiet around here. I'll get Cider and we'll get you first thing in the morning."

"Pastor Moore has already volunteered," Walter pointed out. "I'll tell the others, and we should be there around noon tomorrow."

"Sounds good," said Clayton. "I'll have lunch waiting."

"Okay," said Walter. "You take care. Bye."

"I promise," said Clayton. "See you tomorrow, bye."

Clayton was relieved that the rest of the household would be returning soon. He put another log on the fire and dozed off in his easy chair. When he awoke, the tired man went straight to bed.

Clayton slept long enough to wake up at an ample time. He found the strength to bathe, get into fresh clothing, and make toast for breakfast. He even brewed some coffee and enjoyed a cup with his meal. Feeling a tad better, he thought to himself, *now this is more like it.* Afterward, he started to prepare lunch.

Clayton took the easiness of reheating leftovers by pulling fried chicken, mashed potatoes covered with gravy, and steamed vegetables out of the freezer. It all fit in a cast iron pot. From there, he put it on a back burner and placed the setting on 'low'. That, along with buttered bread, coffee, milk and hot cider would make this warm meal on a cold winter's day irresistible!

When Elizabeth returned home with Walter, Clara and Pastor Moore, she immediately ran up to her papa. Hugging him with all of her might, she said, "I missed you, Papa."

With concern written all over his face, he looked down at her and said, "I heard that you got a little sick and fell down. Are you okay, Elizabeth?"

Looking up at her grandfather she said, "I'm just fine and Clara took really good care of me."

The information brought a sigh of relief, accompanied by a surge of energy. Kissing her on the cheek, he said, "I'm glad to hear that. I missed you too, angel."

The home smelled the way it usually did, with a warm meal in the kitchen and the fireplace casting its flavorful heat. Soon the pastor was leading grace as lunch was blessed. The snow continued to fall outside, and the tradition of the bunkhouse on Coalman's Hill was kept alive.

Later that evening in the living room, Elizabeth got excited and asked if they could all go down the hill on the big sled. The adults saw that such a venture was becoming too much for Clayton and didn't know how to address the little girl. Clara was quick-thinking and spoke up. "Elizabeth, I was hoping that we could work on that afghan we started. When we get it done, we can give it to a needy family to keep them warm."

That sounded good to the seven-year-old. She looked at her papa and asked, "Do you mind if Clara and I work on it, and we can go down the hill another day?"

Clayton was relieved. "Why, sure," he said. "That afghan will make an entire family very happy once you two get it finished."

The granddaughter charged her papa and hugged him with both arms, saying, "Thank you, Papa, thank you!"

All was taken care of as Clara winked at the men. "Elizabeth, I'll make us some hot chocolate," she said in her motherly voice.

"Yippee!" cried out the little girl as she changed directions and hugged Clara.

The three men liked seeing the mother and daughter bond grow before their very eyes. With the two women tied up, an opportunity arose. *Now* would be a good time for Clayton to discuss his future with Walter and Pastor Moore. He looked at his friends and suggested that they meet at the kitchen table.

"I'll make a pot of coffee," said Walter as they all began to move. In moments, they had a private, comfortable setting among friends, away from the granddaughter. The first round was the dicing of shifting eyes to see who would initiate the most sensitive conversation they'd ever share.

The ball was in Clayton's court. He stared straight down to build up the needed courage, and finally broke the ice. "I thank God that I have friends like you," he said in a somber tone.

Two heads nodded behind steaming mugs, but remained silent.

Clayton raised his head. Tears gleamed on his face. He glanced at each friend, then looked up, clasping hands behind his

110

head. Leaning back, he focused into infinity as he spoke. "I asked our Lord to give me more time for Elizabeth's sake. I know that it's a lot to ask, but He has been known to do more than that for others."

Looking at each friend, he said, "I'll try my best to give Him the time needed to accomplish this, while I do my part to help make this happen." He leaned forward, put his elbows on the table and rested his head in opened hands. "If I am not to be granted this," he said in a sniffling, quivering voice, "I will have but no choice to accept our Lord's decision and tell Elizabeth—when I know the time is right."

Three grown men did their best to hold back their tears, but to no avail. Time passed with eyes never meeting, until Pastor Moore said, "That's all you can do, Clayton. Just keep praying."

"Never forget that we're here for you and Elizabeth," said Walter.

What needed to be said was said. More time passed as three teary-eyed men mentally envisioned the bleak future that would undoubtedly unfold. Eventually they started to recover, just as Clara entered the kitchen saying, "I think some hot raspberry cobbler with vanilla ice cream is in order."

"Now *that* sounds good," said Clayton. "Let's *all* enjoy it together in front of the fireplace."

Walter and the pastor were in awe of their friend's spiritual strength. Neither had the energy to talk yet, but both could muster patting him on the back as they carried their mugs to the living room.

Once there, Elizabeth's world took over. "Look, Papa!" she exclaimed. The granddaughter stood back and pointed at the progress she and Clara had made on the afghan. It was beautiful with a series of bright country colors on a white background.

Clayton was taken. "My gosh!" he exclaimed. "Why, you're almost done, and it's so beautiful!" Looking at her gorgeous smile he added, "And it's pretty just like you."

As evening approached, Pastor Moore elected to ride back to the church. "We still have other families there," he explained. "Keep me posted on everything, and always let me know what I can do for you."

111

Clayton cut to the chase and said, "I love you too, Pastor." When the holy man left, Clayton's weak body began to expire. "I need to lie down for a while," he said.

"Don't worry about us," said Walter "There's plenty going on around here to keep us busy. If we don't see you later; we'll see you at breakfast."

"I appreciate that," said Clayton. He approached his little angel and said, "Your papa is going to lie down for a while."

"Are you okay?" she asked with an expression of fear.

Clayton stood straight up and clenched his fists to display toughness. Next he incorporated his fatherly demeanor and cute smile. "I'm just fine," he assured. "It's only a bit of old age, that's all. Now come over here and give me a hug!"

Elizabeth did just that and wrapped both arms around his waist, saying, "I love you, Papa."

The compassionate man swayed back and forth. "I love you too, angel."

Chapter XX

IT WAS NOT BY ACCIDENT that Clayton got up early the next day. He had intentionally gone to bed early the night before to guarantee it. This was done so he could address the day with a running start. The mountain man of Coalman's Hill was determined to prove to the entire household that he was winning the battle to regain his health.

He started his day by looking out his bedroom window to see that the record-setting snowfall had continued. It was evident that the Heavenly crystals had fallen all night. The trees were getting shorter in the snowfields. It was now time to put his best foot forward and show his stuff.

The first thing on his agenda would be to breathe life into the fireplace, brew a pot of coffee then start breakfast. From there he intended to have a day with Elizabeth and even take her sledding.

Things were quite the opposite however, with matters getting worse. Once he took his medicines in the bathroom, he immediately threw up with other horrible symptoms prevalent.

The saintly man, who was trying to prove to God and everyone that he was on the mend, was only fooling himself.

Walter was already up and heard Clayton get sick in the bathroom and return to his room. He gave it a little time, and then went to check up on his friend. In a few minutes, Walter stood outside Clayton's bedroom, softly tapping on his door. "Clayton," he called out quietly, so as not to wake up Clara and Elizabeth. "Are you okay?"

He could hear a multitude of coughing, and then a faint, raspy voice responded. "I'll be fine, Walter. I just need to rest a bit more."

Out of courtesy Walter replied, "Okay," and left.

Later that day, Clara and Elizabeth were working on their project in front of the fireplace. The child inquired at breakfast about her papa. Walter explained that they were up earlier that morning.

"He just needs his rest and will be with us soon," he said in a comforting tone.

Later, her papa did come out of his room, dressed for the day. "How's my little angel?" he asked.

Clayton might have been well-dressed, but his progressing illness was impossible to hide. "Papa," replied the perceptive seven-year-old. "Are you sick? I mean—you don't look well."

Surrounded by the company of adults, he was at a loss for words and stuttered. Finally he said, "Yes, I am sick. But I'm taking good medicine, and we do have the Lord."

Elizabeth started to cry and got up to run to her papa. She hugged him and cried out in a sobbing voice, "I don't want you to die, Papa. I want you to stay here with me."

All he could do was hold her and look at the sad faces of Walter and Clara.

Clayton's wit came to life prompting him to use a hand to raise her chin. While staring at her beautiful eyes he asked, "Aren't I still here with you right now, at this very moment?"

How true. He *was* still there, and that brought comfort to the child—and to the Rodman's. She continued to hold onto her papa, never wanting to let go.

Clayton joined in for the rest of the day and even partook in a board game that night. All was not pleasant, though. There were coughing fits with long visits to the bathroom, and involuntary staggering whenever he walked.

The evening wound down with Clara reading bedtime stories to Elizabeth and the men having a fireside chat. It was there Clayton came to terms with the idea that unless God intervened with a miracle soon, he would be gone in the near future.

"I guess I have no choice but to break it to Elizabeth," he said to Walter.

"If you do leave us," said Walter, "I promise that Clara and I will take care of her and always get her to church."

"I know you will," responded Clayton. "I just wish that I could outlive her, so that she'd always have me," he commented under his breath.

The discussion continued with Clayton asking if he could have some time to be alone with his granddaughter. "That will let me find the right moment to explain all of this to her. If there *is* one..."

It was agreed that the following day, Walter and his wife would take Cider for a sleigh ride to church and stay a night or two. "Remember," said Walter, "We're just a phone call away."

The next day had Clayton doing his very best trying to keep up with Elizabeth. It was moments like watching the snow fall and having hot cocoa together that provided a forgiving pace for him. They got out in the snow briefly and built a snowman.

But upon completing the miniature man with a smiling face made of gravel, Elizabeth fainted.

Clayton recalled that she had fainted the other day and didn't know what to think. He bent over and called out her name. "Elizabeth, darling, are you okay?"

He stared down at her expressionless face. Then her nose started to twitch, and her eyes blinked. "What happened?" she asked in bewilderment. Elizabeth seemed to be fine as she sat up and looked around.

"I don't know," said her papa, "My guess is that all this non-stop activity is starting to catch up to you. Let's go inside and get you warm."

The child and her papa got warm in front of the fire and later shared a frozen pizza for dinner. This particular evening, Elizabeth was the one needing to go to bed first. After watching a little TV in her grandfather's arms, she was already sound asleep. Clayton woke the groggy child and walked her into her bedroom. He tucked Elizabeth in, saying a goodnight prayer as she drifted off to dreamland.

It was now the terminally ill man in his easy chair, staring at the dancing flames before him. Clayton was fully aware that his spiritual request hadn't been answered—*yet.* The tranquil moment required for a heart-to-heart with God Himself existed at that very moment, and Clayton Charles Graves acted on it.

He began to remind the Lord that as always, he'd do whatever He asked of him. The God-fearing man was also quick to let our Creator know that he *never* forgot about the multitude of things He had done for him throughout his life. From there, Clayton reminisced about one blessing after another that saved the day, tragedy that was avoided because of His grace.

As the evening continued, Elizabeth's life took center stage. "Lord, you have been so good about giving her the strength to go on while losing one family member after another," he said. "We realize that all of these wonderful people who've been placed in our lives have been gifts from you. Please understand that regardless, they aren't from *our* family line—and that does make a difference. That child is now down to one last relative. I have to stay around," he pleaded. "I'm the only one she's got left!"

The emotional drain was devouring Clayton as he reached the grand finale. "Please, my Lord, please. Don't let her have a life where she has to continue in this world with no family." Clayton's face was saturated with tears as he concluded his visit with, "Thank you, Lord for hearing my prayers."

Clayton left for his bedroom. Once under the covers, the tired man fell into a deep sleep.

Clayton awoke to a magnificent sunrise. The spectacular array was clearly the most glorious he'd ever seen. The golden rays spread evenly throughout the untouched, glistening hills, as if it were a magic stairway leading to God's kingdom.

He also felt somewhat better and had the strength to put on his bathrobe and go to Elizabeth's room. Upon entering, he saw that an immaculate beam of sunlight was cast over Elizabeth. Its radiant glow seemed focused on the child—who wasn't moving. A feeling came over Clayton as he cautiously walked up to his granddaughter. Her beautiful, innocent face held a partial smile, but there was no sign of breathing.

There was no questioning that the angels had come for Elizabeth. She was now with God, her mother, and those blessed who had gone before.

Clayton remembered his numerous requests to outlive his granddaughter and interpreted this as a punishment. Covering his face with both hands, he cried like a child and bellowed out, "No, my Lord. *This isn't what I meant!*"

Chapter XXI

CLAYTON FELT LIKE HE WAS sentenced to Hell. In his mind, he had greatly exceeded his boundaries with the Lord by having the audacity to interfere with His plans. The living legend of Coalman's Hill was now living his worst fear as if it were a sentence. There was also irony attached—it was exactly what he'd inauspiciously *asked for.*

What Clayton did know was that he was to finish out his life by serving our Heavenly Father—*regardless* of any hardship that lay before him. *I owe it to our Lord to continue being a soldier for Him, without complaining,* concluded Clayton.

There were formalities that needed to be addressed. First and foremost would be to ask God for forgiveness. Next was to call Pastor Moore.

The peaceful look on Elizabeth's face exemplified a good life that had earned a passage to Heaven. That image was the only way Clayton knew his grandchild—it was forever ingrained in his mind, a viewing that did not require a double take. The humbled grandfather sat down at the kitchen table and prayed. It was a short message to our Creator, giving thanks for the wonderful gift that Elizabeth had been for him and to be forgiven for attempting to alter His plans.

With raw courage, he called Pastor Moore and delivered the hard news in a direct fashion, where nothing had to be repeated. The stunned pastor heard it right the first time and paused to let the devastating news register. With all of his strength, he was able to spit out, "Get some rest, Brother Clayton. I'll take care of everything."

Clayton got up and walked around the home to look at his surroundings. Everywhere he looked was a reflection on the beauty Elizabeth had brought into this world. Pictures, artwork, favorite books she liked to have read over and over again, and her ever-present aura filled the bunkhouse.

Bewildered with sadness and unbearable guilt, the lonely grandfather went to his room to lie down. Clayton Graves stared at the ceiling, thinking about the morning's events, and cried. The emotional toll took everything out of the old man, allowing him to have the pleasure of deep sleep.

Hours must have passed. Clayton, who never had to lock the house at night, was gently awoken by Pastor Moore. The holy man was always his bridge of choice to God. Clayton immediately recognized him, and with outstretched arms gave a trembling hug saying, "Elizabeth is gone."

With compassion the pastor said, "We're here to take care of you."

Clayton felt a tingling feeling of relief as he sat up. Realizing that he was loved, he got a surge of energy. "I'll make some coffee," he said.

"That sounds good," replied the pastor. The church leader had a battle on two fronts: He had to comfort his friend and coordinate the mandatory procedures required by the state—all while feeling the loss himself. "Sheriff Gifford is here with the county coroner," said Pastor Moore as he directed business. "This is just a simple process that has to be addressed whenever something like this happens."

Sheriff Will Gifford was a solid friend that Clayton had known for decades. Many time the Scottish descendent sat next to him at a church function or Little League game. The lawman was almost the size of Clayton, with distinct bushy blond hair and blue eyes. He too was a compassionate, God-fearing man who dedicated his life to doing right.

"I don't mind seeing Will on a day like today," Clayton commented. He followed the pastor into the living room and saw the friend who wore a badge. "Good morning, Will. It's always good to see you."

The man holding a white cowboy hat that seemed to come right out of Bonanza said, "We're all so sorry to hear about your little girl."

Clayton's initial shock was over, and he responded, "So am I, but our Lord must have His reasons."

Being the gentleman he was, Will quickly introduced the man next to him. "Clayton, this is Leslie Braxton, our county coroner.

The lean man in a white outfit extended his hand with professionalism. "It's my pleasure to meet you, Mr. Graves. I've heard so much about you."

Leslie Wilson Braxton could have passed for a computer geek. The lanky valedictorian whose white skin could only reflect sunlight stood before Clayton in a business-like manner. Oily brown hair parted to one side and horn-rimmed prescription glasses gave that first impression you could only make once.

It was a given that his off-duty attire would have personified a conservative fashion that went out decades ago. What was important was his demeanor. It was obvious that he was a sensitive, caring soul who belonged there.

Clayton shook his hand and corrected him. "Everyone calls me, Clayton." He said. "It's a pleasure to meet you despite these circumstances, Leslie. Don't worry—I know that you're here to help, and I appreciate that very much."

The lean man peered through his glasses, as his dark eyes dilated. "You certainly live up to your reputation!" complimented the Ivy Leaguer.

Will took over. "Leslie needs to work alone now," he said.

Pastor Moore stepped in and said, "I'll show him where he needs to go." The clergyman left quietly with the coroner following.

"Clayton," said the sheriff. "I hate this part of my job and I promise that it won't take very long. I need to ask you a few questions, if you have time."

"I always have time for you, Will," said Clayton. "I know that you have to do these things."

The two sat down in privacy by the fireplace. With pen and notebook in hand, Will started to ask a few routine questions. They went back and forth, as the sheriff scribbled down a few notes. Finally, Will said, "That's all I need, Clayton." He thanked his friend for his cooperation and again expressed his condolences.

Leaving the residence he said, "I'm also your friend, Clayton—and you know how to get in touch with me."

Pastor Moore was watching from a distance while Leslie performed his duties. The Godly man knew to vacate Clayton from the premises so that he wouldn't see his granddaughter being carted out. "Let's go out back and have coffee in your workshop," he suggested. "We can visit and say some prayers."

A robust cup of coffee with Pastor Moore inside Clayton's man-cave was definitely a more appropriate environment. It momentarily removed him from the surroundings that encompassed Elizabeth's entire life, and surrounded him with his own personal guy stuff. This was the ideal setting for the man who *had* to get away, but couldn't. More importantly, there was no one better to share his guilty feelings with than the preacher who gave him his weekly sermons.

In a short time the men were bundled up and sitting on Clayton's workbench, trying to stay warm. It was a bonus having full mugs of coffee that also served as hand warmers. Already Clayton was showing signs of feeling more at ease. "I certainly appreciate you being here for me—and what you've done so far," he said.

"There is no place I'd rather be than right here with you," came his response.

It was impossible to discuss anything other than the tragedy of Elizabeth's passing. Clayton took no time to expose his great sorrow and reflected on the wonderful life she lived. "That little girl was an angel sent from Heaven. All she did was smile and help everyone," he said through tears. Looking up, he added, "She's back in Heaven with the Lord; just where she came from."

Pastor Moore was in full agreement as he nodded his head. From there, many stories were told by the proud grandfather. Episodes that ranged from helping grownups set up church functions, to her attempts to surprise her papa by making him a home-cooked meal. "She was always thinking about others, but *never* about herself," he pointed out. More stories surfaced about her self-sacrificing, unselfish life. "Once she got money from the tooth fairy and wanted to share it with me," he said.

The tide changed when Clayton openly took full blame for her leaving this world at such a young age. "I had no business whatsoever challenging our Lord to alter His plans for me," he cried out. "Naturally, He'd want her to return to Heaven and be with Him, and my selfish act caused that to happen."

The pastor was glad that Clayton's inner feelings of guilt had finally surfaced. He was patiently waiting to catch it and say something about it. He interjected at that moment with an assertive tone. "I have to disagree with you."

That comment, and who it came from, immediately stopped Clayton in his tracks.

Leaning forward while using his calm voice, the pastor said, "Clayton, we were all praying those very prayers to God, just as you were."

Clayton was dumbfounded and stared back with a blank face.

Pastor Moore continued with his simple genius by making a summary out of it. "Elizabeth's passing is *everyone's* loss."

That thought registered deep with Clayton, giving him a peace within. The men went on for quite a while discussing our Lord's mysterious ways and the *what if's* in life.

Hours passed with the bunkhouse having been vacated long ago. It was getting dark when the pastor suggested that they go inside. "I can even stay here with you, if you'd like," he offered as they entered the wooden fortress.

Clayton requested to be alone that night. The church head had earlier made arrangements for the grieving man to have his options. He thoughtfully had Sheriff Will Gifford and Coroner Leslie Braxton follow him in the county's search and rescue sled. This gave him the option to stay as long as Clayton needed him without infringement.

The pastor walked up to the fireplace and threw in a few dry logs. "I'll continue to pray for you and your little girl tonight," he said.

"Thanks, pastor," replied Clayton. "I now know that my praying was the right thing to do, and I'll keep praying all night long until I fall asleep."

Chapter XXII

THE NEWS TRAVELED FAST with the aid of cell phones, mail carriers, barber shops and grocery clerks. Within a day, the entire community and outlying areas knew about the little girl on Coalman's Hill.

The hardest hit was the bunkhouse and the church that led to it. Pastor Moore utilized all of his strength to remain composed as he guided the congregation through the devastating loss. "Everything is in the Lord's hands," he would announce repetitively throughout the humble church.

Clara Rodman had to step up as well. She was specifically chosen by children of all ages as Elizabeth's special friend. They were now sharing their first crisis together and needed her. "The pastor's right," she would say as a cluster of sobbing youth gathered around her. "God *is* in control, and He's taking care of all of us— including Elizabeth."

Marlene and Jolene Johnson looked at their mother figure and asked, "Where is Elizabeth right now?" The old woman instinctively wrapped her arms around them and said in a calm, laughing voice, "With our Lord, of course - and she's very happy."

The eight-year-old twins dropped their jaws, and with eyes wide open began to jump up and down, asking, "Can I go, can I go? Please!"

Clara Rodman continued to laugh as she said, "We all want to go, but must wait our turn."

"Will we get to see her again?" asked Phillip Rozier. The den mother had an answer for the timid, red-headed second grader.

"Yes," she replied with her loving eyes. "We will all get to see her again when we meet God." Her encouragement was heard by the many who surrounded her turning saddened faces into smiles.

Turning on a dime, she placed a look of elation across her face and asked the children, "Hey, do we want to perform a play to honor Elizabeth and make everyone happy? Let's take a vote," she suggested. "All in favor, raise your hand."

Clara immediately raised her hand as her following did the same. It was unanimous. Cheers filled the room. "Okay," she said. "First, we need to pick a story we want to do. Does anyone have any ideas?"

All hands went up with each and every child's opinion taken into consideration. The children couldn't help but love the good woman. They knew that with her *everyone* was important!

Pastor Moore watched the makeshift pep rally with Walter. "This church certainly needs her," he commented.

"The whole world needs her," added Walter.

Clayton Grave's privacy was respected by the entire community. It was understood that it was best to have Pastor Moore designated as the only one who would make contact during the first trying days. "He just needs some time to himself, and to be alone with God," he would tell the parishioners. "I'll let you know if he needs anything," he would add.

Clayton appreciated the immense consideration he was given. His request was to be left alone for a short period—and that included gifts, flowers, or even a card. "I just want things around here to remain the same," he said.

Everyone was aware with permission granted.

Clayton's plan was to have a sit-down with Leslie Braxton once his report was complete. The protective grandfather needed to know if he was guilty of any negligence that could have saved her. His plan was to have Leslie invited to her memorial service and confer with him earlier in the day. Pastor Moore understood Clayton's wishes and called Leslie. The county coroner expressed that he planned on being there regardless, and looked forward to meeting with Clayton. "I will have my report concluded within two days," he said.

That information allowed for arrangements to be made for the memorial service. A brief discussion with Clayton pinpointed that there was plenty of time to make preparations for the upcoming Sunday at twelve noon.

Everyone was determined to give without interfering with Clayton's privacy. It was agreed that worthy causes throughout the county would receive donations in honor of his little angel.

During the week, prayer services were held that accepted donations to be spread throughout the community—gifts that honored Elizabeth by spreading goodwill in her name. At her viewing, over one hundred thank-you cards were placed in front of her casket. The cards went into detail about how Elizabeth Graves' life had put food on a table or paid an electric bill.

While looking at the face that held a loving glow, her papa thought to himself, *You're back with our Lord, and still you are helping others and making them happy.*

On Sunday morning, Clayton Graves dressed in his favorite suit—a sharp black three-piece with a 'dignitary' red tie—one that he would only wear at weddings, religious holidays, and memorial services. The ceremonial suit he wanted to be buried in.

Looking like the king of the world, he sat in the very room where he had visited with Dr. Schoenberg not long ago. This time it was for a more important issue: to get answers about the dearest person he had ever loved.

Facing him was the coroner, who was at a loss for words. The passive figure felt out of his element not knowing how to begin addressing such a great man on such a personal subject.

Clayton's years of guiding young men into battle came into play. He would simply use the direct approach and efficiently take care of business. In a clear tone, he said, "You mentioned that your report would be finished. If it is, could you tell me what you found?"

Coroner Leslie Braxton perked up, adjusted his glasses and answered the call. "I'm afraid that your daughter, Elizabeth had Brugada Syndrome.

Clayton's face contorted as he digested a word that he'd never heard before.

"Brugada Syndrome?" he asked while leaning forward.

Leslie went on to explain about the rare syndrome that is normally found in Asia among men; an almost unheard-of condition that had been known to leave its mark in this country.

This was all new to Clayton who asked, "What are the symptoms of this condition?"

"That's the problem," replied the coroner. "Basically, there aren't any, with the exception of blacking out unexpectedly. From there, it is known to sneak up on its victims when they are asleep— and take them."

Clayton started to reflect on the information and realized that his little girl was starting to black out without any pain. It was also a fact that his granddaughter did indeed lose her life while in the comfort of sleep.

"Could she have caught this from me or anyone else?" he asked in fear.

"No," answered Leslie. "This is a condition that a person can only be born with that basically goes undetected until it's too late.

Leslie Braxton stood up and tried to make more sense out of it by finding the right analogy. He began to pace back and forth, nervously adjusting his glasses. In a futile effort, he raised a finger high in the air and started to spit out words while staring at the carpet. "Well, you see... Well, you see..."

Clayton was relieved to find that his granddaughter was genuinely a victim of circumstances. That, along with his constant prayers and contact with Pastor Moore, had him feeling better. There was also a service to take place shortly, prompting this meeting to come to a close. Having the good man sized up, he thought he'd speed things along by tossing in a fish.

"Is it like a car?" he asked.

The light bulb inside Leslie's head turned on as he spun around, pointing at Clayton. "That's it!" he exclaimed. "It's like a car!"

Without interruption, the coroner went into 'automatic' and graced the mountain man with his insight on life and automobiles.

Chapter XXIII

THE MEMORIAL SERVICE for Elizabeth Graves exemplified the grace of her soul. Amazingly, the record-setting snow fall held up all day, from the start of the procession to the burial.

The all-day event was decorated with lavish floral displays and pictures that choreographed her short life. Favorite hymns were sung throughout the ceremony, and stories were shared. It appeared that every member of the community attended, along with those who had never met her, but received a donation in her memory. Old friends who had moved long ago were also present. Introductions were made, followed by intense hugging and tears. Every available fold-up chair had to be used.

This was undoubtedly the most important day in the history of Freeland, with Clayton Graves being a proud man. He thanked everyone for being there and for always making his little angel happy.

The closure for Elizabeth Marie Graves' life was nothing short of a slice of Heaven.

It was days after Elizabeth's ceremony when a lone Clayton Graves visited his family plot. This was his first visit since Sunday as the grieving man's health continued on a downward spiral. He was now utilizing a walking stick he made as a child, and coughed up blood more frequently.

Bundled up in loose clothing, he looked down at the newly placed granite marker. Already, it was snow-covered and blended in with the others. The former military man took a step back and inspected the regimented formation where his family was buried. All was lined up in a neat and orderly fashion, with his cherished granddaughter lying next to her mother and grandmother. Next to his wife and abreast with his parents was a designated vacant space.

Clayton nodded as he looked at his future site. He said softly, "I guess it will be my turn next."

Out of nowhere came the only voice that could accompany him at a time like this. "You're absolutely right," commented Pete Rainwater.

Clayton immediately responded without a flinch. "I was waiting for you this time, so you didn't scare me."

"Do you realize what's happening here?" asked the Native.

Pete Rainwater always had an uncanny knack for popping up out of nowhere to relay his wisdom at the right time. Clayton was in great pain and knew that Pete would shed light on the big picture. Motioning with his hands, he encouraged his wise friend to continue.

"Tell me," came Clayton's quick reply.

"You got your lifelong wish, Brother!" proclaimed Pete.

Clayton winced, showing confusion on his face. He shook his head, saying, "I don't understand."

Pete stood in front of him with arms stretched out and began to explain. "Our prayers are all on the same wavelength, my friend. It's just like this mountain. All news is meant for everybody—and it travels."

"You have always prayed to be there for your family, and to protect them," he said. "You actually lived to watch over all of us—including your soldiers on the battlefield. In fact, you were even looking after the enemy soldiers as well, because I can *feel* that you didn't want to harm any of them. You just wanted to show them our ways. My gut feeling tells me that many of them went on to have good lives by becoming American citizens, all because of one Commander Graves."

Tears flowed down Clayton's face. For decades he lived as a silent war hero who used the grace of prayer to engage in battle. It was the ultimate honor—one that didn't require a medal. It was an accomplishment of grace and valor that allowed him to receive the highest gift: being able to live with himself. At last, the former commander who lived in the hills had someone vindicate him for serving our Lord on the battlefield. The retired soldier stood tall and puffed out his chest.

Pete had more.

"Every person you have ever met was blessed, and *that's* why you were placed here," he said, pointing at him. "You were *always* praying for others, and you asked the Lord to allow you to be what was needed of you to help others. Over and over your prayers were virtually asking God to allow you to see your entire family through—by outliving them."

It was now the crucial moment as his fellow mountain man put the icing on the cake. Pete leaned forward, placing his hands above his knees, and spoke. "It's your turn now," he said. "That little granddaughter of yours was committed to leave us at a young age, so that *you* could be the last one off the battlefield. God gave each of you a terminal condition that made no sense whatsoever. She was to leave just before you did, because you completed your job down here."

"Ya got your wish, Brother Clayton; but there is something else you need to realize." Pete took a deep breath and said, "There is a reason why the Rodmans are staying with you. That woman needs to go on and take care of the many children who were guided to her. She always wanted to be a mother and never knew that she was destined to be one at an older age—when she was needed most. It's a calling to keep the doors of that old bunkhouse open with the love of God always flowing."

Clayton looked at the headstones that surrounded him, knowing that each lived a life devoted to serving God. He also knew that they did received their final reward—living in harmony with Him. True, he had to encounter the pain of having them go before him. But still, they did carry out our Lord's will and left this world a better place.

It now made sense why a man with no vices had mysteriously become stricken with an incurable cancer: his little girl was taken during the night due to a rare, undetectable condition.

Clayton realized that this was all God's plan, and that every member of his family had made the grade. His final battle in life was won with all of his soldiers accounted for. It was time for Commander Clayton Charles Graves to 'bring up the rear' and come home. He would soon join all of the friends and family he helped until their dying day. The gates were indeed beginning to open for the Mountain Man of Coalman's Hill, passage to our Lord's kingdom where he would be united with his wife, parents, daughter, childhood friends and little Elizabeth. In true fashion, he could live out eternity by helping our Heavenly Father watch over others and give that *extra push* when allowed.

The dying man felt free as he raised his arms in the air and turned in circles. For the first time in his life, Clayton *wanted* to die.

He turned to thank Pete for his hindsight—but the compassionate soul was already gone without a trace.

Chapter XXIV

CLAYTON HAD ONE LAST CHORE to fulfill before leaving this world. It would be to carry on the tradition of the legendary bunkhouse by having it willed to his friends, Walter and Clara. "Those children need you," he explained to Clara.

After their parting, it was put in writing that the church would be the final heirs. "We can laugh about the good times we had down here," said a jubilant Clayton as he signed the documents. "When we're not swapping stories, I'll introduce you to our *new* family," he added.

Walter and his wife had visits with Dr. Schoenberg and Leslie Braxton. They, along with Pastor Moore, allowed them to accept the loss of Elizabeth and the failing condition of her grandfather. They were encouraged by all, including Clayton, to look ahead and proudly accept the challenges God had in store for them.

On that note, the couple felt like they just graduated from high school—with their entire future to look forward to! Though bittersweet, there was an element of thrill knowing that they would finally have the children that were *meant* for them. It would be a changing of the guards on Coalman's Hill, with Walter and Clara being handed the torch.

Clayton was of sound mind and tactfully hinted that he would like to stay alone in the bunkhouse and be close to the Lord.

"I don't mind you checking up on me every few days," he said. "It's just that I want to be alone with my bible and settle down where I was raised."

The old home was basically a hospice where Clayton would finish out his life alone. "Sure," came Walter's reply as he gently shook Clayton's weakened shoulder. "We'll give you a call every few days, and might even drop by once a week."

Clayton appreciated how easy Walter and his wife made the situation. Their parting was nothing more than a handshake with a few spoken words. It was a nonchalant affair that suggested they would be seeing their friend many more times.

The old man recently moved his bed into the living room so that he could enjoy the warmth of the fireplace and gaze out the window. He also took the famed timepiece and tacked it on the wall next to his bed, and propped up the record-setting sled by the door to savor his triumph. Surrounded by pictures of his family with bible in hand, Clayton was at peace. More importantly, he was not disturbed. Everyone knew of the dying man's last request and respected it.

Day by day, his condition worsened rapidly. Clayton grew weaker to where his hobbling caused immense dizziness and pain. His final days had him limited to brief visits to the bathroom and eventually no appetite for food. Soon it took all of his strength to place a log on the fire.

It was a crystal-clear night with glistening stars above when the world changed. Our Heavenly Father waved His majestic hand summoning angels to bring "Papa" home.

That evening the bedridden man was hoping that sleep would relieve the agony he felt throughout his body. All at once, Clayton's energy level began to pulsate and became rejuvenated. He was full of energy and felt an enthusiasm that had left him when he was a child. He sat up with vigor and looked out the window. There before his very eyes were telltale signs of old friends prancing around. A showering of gleaming snow coming from all directions told the story. Furthermore, it was concentrated by the old stump where his friends always gathered—the very signature that could only come from those who always played there.

Leaning on the wall next to him, he lifted the stopwatch off the tack it hung from. He pointed to himself with pride and proudly waved the recorded time for all to see. The reigning King

Of Coalman's Hill himself had no doubt that soon he'd be in the midst of things, playing with his friends.

Childhood memories surfaced of the many times Clayton had seen them outside frolicking in the snow; moments that made the anxious child don winter apparel and grab his sled, events that represented some of the happiest times of his life.

The dying man remembered his mother's immortal words when she referred to their front door as *the gates of Heaven*. Looking over, he could see the classic Flexible Flyer poised once again to do battle—this time for eternity.

Golden strings started to fill his world as choirs of angels serenaded him. The music carried the voice of his mother, with Elizabeth calling out, "Come home, Papa!"

The child inside Clayton was alive and well. The energetic boy who lived to pray and play would soon be dragging the Graves Express out the front door for a final time. But first, he must get his rest and fall asleep.

Knowing that the red glow in the fireplace would be sufficient enough to keep him warm, he looked outside one last time. To his delight, the weather had changed. A few snowflakes had transcended into another flurry. At peace, he clutched his bible while still holding onto the stopwatch, and snuggled under the quilt. It was the most relaxed state he had ever felt in his entire life. In peace, the servant gradually drifted off with a feeling of *knowing*.

Soon, Clayton Charles Graves would be walking through the gates of Heaven to meet our Lord—a crossing that secures a home in God's kingdom with loved ones ever-present.

The place where prayers are answered, snow is abundant...and there's no school.

The End

Epilogue

THE LIFE OF CLAYTON GRAVES reflected the values by which we are taught to live. Prayer and good will to our fellow man was his trademark with *every* meal being a Thanksgiving all in its own. Most of all, he personified the epitome of life by having an unconditional *mother's love* for all.

A love that demanded he see his entire family through, without ever leaving anyone behind.

His acts of humanity were spread throughout his entire life, but nowhere were they more prevalent than in the love he showed raising his granddaughter. A little girl who had everything a child could ever want, *because of him.*

There was more to him than being a good family man, church goer and neighbor. Commander Clayton Charles Graves was also a patriot who served his country as a career, the soldier who approached battle in prayer and never lost a man.

Clayton Graves couldn't smile unless he was sharing with others. Even when his life was deteriorating through a painful, incurable disease, he still put others first. It would be an understatement to say Clayton Graves was unselfish. After all, how could a devout servant of our Lord be anything less than giving?

It served as testimony that he never once claimed ownership of the fabled bunkhouse until it was time to sign it over to Walter and Clara Rodman. This was an elderly couple that had a void to fill by never having children of their own. Fate intervened when they lost their home, with Clayton coming to the rescue. The good man *knew* it was a calling by our Lord and naturally insisted they take up residency with him and his granddaughter, a welcomed addition that kept the structure's tradition alive. This couple would go on to finish out their lives by maintaining the same prayer-filled, open-door policy that always existed—one that included many children who *needed* them.

Throughout the book, Clayton refers to the legendary bunkhouse where he lived as 'God's house'.

How right he was...

It was basically a place of refuge that blossomed into a sanctuary for those who were mysteriously led there. It was a shelter way up in the mountains that served as a beacon for all to see.

This book is all about what a family can have if their door is left open with a few prayers thrown in—the very formula with which Clayton Graves was raised. And he had an understanding with our Creator that he carried throughout life.

His reward?

In the end, Clayton was blessed by being granted his life-long wish.

Like his soldiers, he was allowed to leave this world knowing all of his family was accounted for — with *no one* left behind.

Matt Shea

Author Biography

MATT SHEA IS A DEVELOPING AUTHOR, having published eight books. He is greatly inspired by the writings of Andy Griffith and focuses on the common folk small towns are made of.

He credits the success of his first book, "The Groundskeeper And Other Short Stories," to his family. The values instilled throughout his childhood gave him the strong sense of justice that is conveyed in his writings. The Shea family is only an average American family from an average neighborhood. Their secret is that they are close knit and accept others.

Matt's mother, Vyerl, set an example of being self-sacrificing, having never placed herself first. She always cared about the feelings of others, no matter who they were. She even sponsored many foster children, despite having a family of eight. During the holidays, the Roman Catholic mom had been known to have a Hanukkah bush for their Jewish friends. There were even years when the family would make Christmas gifts and personally deliver them to seniors in rest homes.

Many of Matt's friends are senior citizens or foreign born. He has the common practice of brewing a pot of tea and inviting them over to watch Alfred Hitchcock. Together they will watch Hitchcock, share a cup of tea, and afterwards listen to his manuscripts. Sometimes these social gatherings last well beyond midnight.

"This is where I get most of my ideas," says Matt. "I learned this from my mom."

Matt Shea appreciates all who take the time to read his stories. He even has a site where many free stories in their entirety are available and extends his email address for those who have any comments or ideas. Matt knows that through other people, he can expand as a writer and a person.

Matt Shea
www.mattsheabooks.com
www.worknmatt7@aol.com

Laura Shea with her dad, author Matt Shea.